Whateverland

by

Zackary Richards

Ari Publishing

Chapter 1

"Had that dream about the two angels again," I said to my daughter as I shuffled through the kitchen. Getting no response, I shrugged, shook my head and continued on, past the living room and into the bathroom for my morning whiz.

As she placed my breakfast on the table, my beloved daughter Turtledove turned and said, "You realize nobody gives a damn, don't you?" Waving her off, I closed the bathroom door behind me.

At 6'4'' and 200 lbs. of solid muscle, Turtledove's quite the imposing figure, particularly in her Homeland Security body armor, steel-toed boots and her jet-black hair tied up in a bun.

Frankly, she's scary as hell.

In the living room, my four-year-old grandson, Bosco O'Bama the Third, sat in my recliner doing *The New York Times* crossword puzzle on his electronic tablet.

I hate my life.

"Make sure you take him to the park; put him on the swings and shit," Turtledove called out as she went through her daily routine of shoving her peanut butter and jelly sandwiches into a paper bag and pouring coffee into her thermos. "And run him around so he'll be worn out when I get home from work," she added raising her voice over the din of the flushing toilet. "Oh, and don't go filling his head with that loony-toon nonsense you fed me when I was a kid. He should have at least some chance of growing up normal."

After washing and drying my hands, I left the bathroom and entered the kitchen. "Shouldn't he be in pre-school, or kindergarten or Harvard?" I asked, taking a

1

moment to sniff the aroma of freshly brewed coffee. "He's smart enough."

"Well, that's the problem," she said, grabbing my shoulders and shoving me into a chair at the kitchen table. "He's too damn smart. If he took after your side of the family instead of Mom's, he'd be riding the short bus to school like his Gam'pa did.

I couldn't help but grin. She said Gam'pa intentionally because that's the way Bosco O'Bama the Third pronounces it. I love it when he calls me Gam'pa

Turtledove slapped a fork, a spoon and an assortment of pills on the checkered tablecloth, then stepped back, folded her arms and said, "Now eat your breakfast and take your meds."

"What is this slop on my plate?" I asked, looking down at godknowswhat. "It looks like you emptied the garbage disposal on it."

"Just eat it," she snapped. "It's brain food."

"Who's brain?" I snarled as I pushed the plate away.

She pulled her Glock 9. "I said. Eat it!"

I growled, picked up my fork, stabbed whatever that green shit was and begrudgingly stuffed it into my mouth. "You know, if you hadn't hid my shotgun," I said between chews, "you'd be picking up what remained of your head about now."

"Yeah, well, that's why I hid it," she replied, holstering her pistol. She walked to the living room doorway and called out. "Bosco, your breakfast is ready."

Moments later, Bosco O'Bama the Third skipped into the kitchen and took a seat at the table. I love that little scamp with his big round head, red-hair and freckles.

2

"Hey!" I said, pointing to his bowl, "how come he gets Captain Canaveral Sugar Corn Squares and I get puke du jour?"

"Because," she growled between clenched teeth as she poured milk into his cereal, "he's a healthy, growing boy and you're a rancid old fart who should have kicked off years ago."

"Mother, please," Bosco said gently taking her hand. "You shouldn't admonish Gam'pa for not being dead. It's your gentle, caring devotion to him and our family that has added years to his life. Seriously, Mother, without you, Gam'pa's diet would consist of nothing but Jack Daniels, pizza and bacon slathered in mayonnaise."

"You're damn right it would!" I said as I spit out something that resembled a ballbearing.

Turtledove grew misty and brushed back a tear. "You're right, honey. My problem is that I love too much!"

"Your problem is you're a fucking gigantosaurus with the personality of a wolverine." I replied.

She reached for her gun, but Bosco stayed her hand. "Now, now, Mother. Like you always say, Gam'pa's brain functions much like a clogged toilet, so patience and understanding must come to the fore."

Turtledove bowed her head and nodded. "You're right. We all share some responsibility for your grandfather's continued presence."

"Speaking of continued presences, shouldn't you be hitting the road?" I said with a quick tilt of my head toward the door.

She cocked a fist and stormed over. "You'll be hitting the linoleum if you keep running your mouth, old man!"

3

Later, after Turtledove left for work and I found my way to my living room recliner, Bosco O'Bama the Third, dressed in blue jeans, a red flannel shirt and high-top sneakers climbed into my lap and said, "Gam'pa, Mother said I take after Gam'ma's side of the family. What was she like and how did you meet?"

"Well, son," I replied, placing my hand on his shoulder, "it all began one summer evening. The night air was intoxicating, the streets were electric with excitement, neon signs flashed, music poured from nightclubs and I just knew something great was about to happen. I had all of my teeth in those days and most of my marbles, and as I made my way through the streets of Greenwich Village, I saw a poster outside a strip club called Uncle Spanky's. The poster was of their featured performer, a statuesque woman with flowing black hair, sparkling blue eyes, a terrific figure, and a peg leg. She was billed as 'Thumpie the Love Pirate'. Under that it read, 'She'll steal your heart!' Intrigued and being quite the dancer myself, I entered, took a seat and awaited her performance.

"Suffice it to say, I was not disappointed. As the lights went down and the curtain went up, the audience lit up with excitement as Thumpie leapt into the spotlight and performed her sultry seductive dance while playing the squeezebox. I was captivated by her bouncing yabows as she clog-danced across the stage.

"I knew then I had to make her mine.

"We dated for a while and I finally convinced her to quit Uncle Spanky's and join me on the clog-dancing circuit. We were an overnight sensation. As we clogged our way across America, the audience would applaud and sing, "Thumpity, thump, thump, thumpity thump, thump, look at Thumpie go. Life was good."

4

"But Gam'pa," Bosco said with a puzzled expression, "Mother says you were a rock and roll star. She made no mention of your clog-dancing success."

I nodded. "That's true. I was forced into rock and roll stardom when, during one of our clog-dancing extravaganzas, tragedy struck."

Bosco took my arm as his eyes widened. "Oh no! What happened?"

I studied the floor. "Well… your grandmother and I were performing at Shea Stadium before 55,000 rabid fans. The cops were straining to hold back the crowds of screaming teenagers as your grandmother went into her clog-dancing finale. She was spinning and doing her high kick, when suddenly, her peg leg flew off, hit some kid in the back of the head, sending him and his wheelchair tumbling down the stairs just as the crowd was chanting the thumpity thump, thump..."

"Oh, my!"

"It was a disaster," I said solemnly. "We cancelled the rest of our tour and waited for the prognosis. Well," I said, brushing back a tear, it wasn't good. Turns out the damage to the wheelchair was irreparable, and if the boy wanted to go somewhere, he'd have to get up off his ass and walk, or at the very least, buy another wheelchair."

"How tragic!" Bosco commented, showing heartfelt concern. "What happened then?"

"Well," I said, as I took out a handkerchief and blew my nose, "your grandmother was so grief stricken she never clog-danced again, and since I had become addicted to crowd adulation and strippers, I reluctantly became a world-famous rock star."

5

Forgetting Bosco was in my lap, I jumped to my feet. "Enough with the sad stories," I said as he tumbled to the floor, "let's go outside and have some fun!"

Chapter 2

"I wish you'd stop. Just quit once and for all," Anne said sourly as her sister Eleanor lit a cigarette. They were sitting at the kitchen table at their father's house, the house they'd grown up in, nursing their respective coffees.

With her elbow on the table and her hand stuffed deep inside her shoulder-length curly brown hair, thirty-one-year-old Eleanor, wearing a gray hoodie and blue jeans, exhaled a long stream of smoke toward the ceiling, shrugged, rolled her eyes and tapped the cigarette on the ashtray. "Why should I quit? So I can wind up like Dad? We all have to croak sooner or later, and I'd much rather go quick with a heart attack or a stroke than waste away like him." She tilted her head to the bedroom down the hall.

"It's not the same, and you know it, Elle," Anne replied, lifting her coffee cup to take a sip. She was a tall, attractive woman, with sparkling green eyes and full lips. Her long blond hair was pulled back in a tight bun. There was a gold detective badge on the belt of her beige pants and a sharp crease under the left arm of her black blouse, created by her police issue automatic, now locked inside her car.

In her father's present condition, having a loaded firearm within arm's reach was not a good idea. "It's bad enough we have to take care of Dad," she said. "I sure as hell don't want to take care of you when we're Dad's age."

They both turned when Mrs. Tuttle, their father's caregiver, entered the room.

"How's he doing?" Eleanor asked, crushing out her cigarette and waving away the smoke. Anne placed her coffee cup down.

"Same as yesterday," Mrs. Tuttle replied, solemnly shaking her head. There was a hard look on the forty-five-year-old woman's face. Her short, graying hair, black eyebrows and olive complexion revealed a lifetime of service. Although only 5'5", she was in excellent shape from lifting patients and placing them in wheelchairs, baths, etc. She drew a breath. "I don't like saying this but I don't think he'll come out of it this time."

Anne scowled. "Why not? He's snapped out of these spells before."

Mrs. Tuttle again shook her head. "It's been nearly three months since he's had both feet in the real world. Sometimes... well..."

As Anne waved her hand dismissively, Eleanor rose and calmly said, "What makes you think he's reached that point?"

"Anybody care for tea?" Mrs. Tuttle asked as she walked to the stove, shook the teakettle and hearing water sloshing inside, placed it on the burner and turned it on.

Seeing both women shaking their heads regarding the offer, she returned, dropped into a seat at the table, placed her elbow on the floral placemat and laid her chin on her hand. "A doctor once told me the brain is like a computer, and like a computer, when the brain contracts a virus, the information it stores becomes corrupted, causing a number of completely unrelated files, that is, memories to merge. In your father's case the neurovirus causes him to remember parts of one memory, but because the rest no longer makes sense, his brain reconfigures it into something completely unrelated."

Anne eyed her. "Put that in English."

Mrs. Tuttle nodded. "All right. Many years ago, I was taking care of an elderly woman named Agnes Beau who

8

insisted the pizza delivery boy was her long, departed husband, James. The boy looked nothing like him but she was adamant. It took several weeks before I noticed the name of the pizzeria on the box was Jimbo's"

"Ahh," Anne said, "James Beau, Jimbo. I get it."

"So why does this happen?" Elle asked. She felt a sudden chill so she sat back down and zipped her hoodie.

The tea kettle whistled and steam poured from its spout. Mrs. Tuttle rose, turned off the gas and poured the boiling water over the tea bag in the cup. "It's like this," she said, placing the kettle on the back burner. "Dementia is like drowning and memories are like slowly disappearing floatation devices. In desperation, the patient grabs whatever recollections remain to form some hybrid raft to keep their illusions afloat. But as those memories fade, they inevitably succumb."

Anne said. "But Dad doesn't have dementia or Alzheimer's, so you can't…" she stopped and let out a sigh. A moment later she nodded and continued. "Okay, I see your point. The damage caused by the viral infection makes him act like a dementia patient, so I guess it *is* possible he's experiencing similar symptoms. If that's the case, just how much time do you figure he has?" Anne asked, biting her lower lip.

Mrs. Tuttle's face became hard, like a person mustering their courage to perform an unpleasant task. She removed the tea bag, squeezed it and placed it on the floral painted saucer and returned to the table. "I'm no doctor, but in my twenty-five years of working with people like your father," she said, not looking at either of her employers, "it's clear to me that those moments when he recognizes you both and can hold a conversation are coming to an end."

9

Knowing that Anne would likely demand an explanation, Mrs. Tuttle added, "He's starting to notice that his personal effects are disappearing, and because he can't remember what happened to them, he'll suspect we're stealing them. Shortly after that, he'll think we're holding him against his will because he'll forget he lives here. And when that time comes, he's going to need around-the-clock care."

"You're talking about a nursing home?" Eleanor asked.

Mrs. Tuttle shook her head. "I'm talking about hospice," she said, then took a sip of her unsweetened tea.

*

"What are we going to do first, Gam'pa?" Bosco O'Bama the Third asked as we walked out the back door and onto the deck.

The sun had started its trek across a sky filled with cottony clouds, and the air was brisk enough to get a person's morning engines started. The boy formed a visor with his hand, placed it to his forehead and stared out at the vast amusement park behind my house that was Whateverland. Center stage and standing mightily above the rest, was the Ferris wheel with the word **Whateverland** majestically lettered in neon tubing in its center. The other spectacular lights embedded on it were unlit since it was daytime, but even without them, the reflective steel structure was an impressive sight. Giraffes and elephants roamed freely in the distance and the tall spires and wind turbines towered over Land o' the Future.

"First, we check the animals in the Land o' Jungles," I replied, placing my foot on the fence and tightening the laces on my hiking boots. "Make sure they're all right. Then if we have time, we'll go on a few of the rides."

10

Bosco, wearing his blue windbreaker, beamed and spun in a circle with his arms extended. "Oh, that's great; I love the rides, especially the guitar boat. What inspired you to build this remarkable place?"

"Well, when you're a rock star, it's kind of expected," I said with a shrug as I slid my hands into the pockets of my jeans, walked down the three wooden steps and set out with my grandson toward the large silver entry gates of my personal amusement park.

"Elvis started it with Graceland and Michael Jackson continued the tradition with Neverland, so I felt it was my responsibility to build Whateverland."

"Why did you name it Whateverland, Gam'pa?" the boy asked as he snapped a twig from a bush and began peeling the bark as we walked.

I sorted through my recollections. "When construction began here on August Mountain," I said, "the press was asking what I was going to put in it. I had no idea, so I always replied, "Oh, whatever. So, not having anything to work with, the press began calling it Whateverland and the name stuck. And since I…"

I stopped, shook my head in annoyance and put my hands on my hips. "That damn elephant!"

Bosco eyed me then turned to see what I was looking at. "Gam'pa, what's…?"

I pointed to the Joshua tree at the far end of the property. "It's Gladys. She snuck out of the Land o' Jungles and is up in the tree again."

Bosco strained to see. "Gladys is in that tree? Elephants can't climb trees."

I rolled my eyes and shook my head. Youth always think they know everything.

11

As we drew closer and entered the tree's shadow, I pointed at Gladys and said, "Well then, how do you explain that?"

Bosco slid his hands into the back pockets of his jeans and drew a breath. "I can't. However, I suspect this might be a psychotic episode brought on by the trauma of being your grandson."

"I am not a figment of your imagination, young man," Gladys said sternly.

Bosco's eyes widened and his jaw dropped.

"What did I tell you about climbing trees?" I said, calling to her. Admittedly, my tone was harsh, but I was tired of her foolishness.

Gladys wrapped her trunk around a lower branch and swung down. As she dropped in front of me—and the dirt and dust flew—she said, "You're not being fair. Rosencrantz and Guildenstern do it all the time and you never yell at them."

"Rosencrantz and Guildenstern are monkeys. Monkeys belong in trees. Elephants do not," I replied brushing the dust off the sleeves of my jacket.

"You men are all alike," she spat. "Always trying to keep women from doing the things they love."

"That's not it at all."

I noticed Bosco O'Bama the Third staring gap-jawed at us both. I must try to remember that it upsets children when adults argue.

"Oh, no? Then explain why the monkeys are allowed to play in the trees but I'm not. I'm just as good at climbing as they are."

I rolled my eyes and placed my hands on my hips. I hate having these arguments with her. "Even if that were

12

true, monkeys have opposable thumbs and tails and are proportionally fitted to swing in trees."

Gladys's eyes widened. "Proportionally fitted!? Are you saying I'm fat?! Is that it?!!"

I had gone too far. I had forgotten this was Gladys's time of the month and how sensitive she became and tried to backpedal but I had boxed myself into a corner.

Gladys took two steps back. "That's it, isn't it?" she said as tears formed in her eyes. "You think I'm too fat to play in the trees. That's cruel. Yes, I'll admit I've been hitting the donut cart a bit more than usual recently but I've been lonely and out of sorts. Besides," she added as her anger returned, "you would never tell Cissy she was too fat!"

Bosco turned to me. "Who's Cissy?"

"She's the blue whale in the lake," I replied, tilting my head in its direction. "And the reason I would never say that to Cissy," I said turning back to Gladys, "is because Cissy isn't crazy enough to climb trees!"

With that, Gladys burst into tears and ran off.

"Ah, nuts!" I said, disgusted with myself. It was then I noticed that Bosco was checking his pulse, then closing his eyes and touching his nose with his index fingers.

"What are you doing?" I asked.

"Just trying to ascertain the extent of this psychotic episode I appear to be having," he replied as he pressed his index finger to his wrist. "I wonder if I've suffered brain damage."

"Don't worry," I said patting the boy on the back as we resumed walking. "Insanity doesn't run in our family, although admittedly, it does walk at a brisk pace. C'mon, let's see how the rest of the animals are doing."

13

Chapter 3

That evening, Mrs. Tuttle, having served her charge his dinner and seeing him off to his daily strolls around the spacious back yard, gathered her things and prepared to leave. She had placed a warm bowl of spaghetti on the table with two plates and silverware, along with crystal glasses, an open bottle of wine and rolls and butter. As she headed for the door, she took a quick peek out the back and felt pride at having successfully guided him through another day.

"It looks delicious, Mrs. Tuttle. Thank you." Anne commented as she and her sister took their seats at the kitchen table. "I was just thinking, with Dad's sense of humor and creativity, this imaginary world he's creating is probably a fun place."

Mrs. Tuttle was putting on her coat but upon hearing this, drew a hard breath through clenched teeth then slowly let it out. "In these situations, humor and creativity are rarely a good thing." She momentarily fumbled with her coat zipper before getting it to work.

Concern crossed Eleanor's face as she rose from the table, opened a drawer under the sink and pulled a folded cloth from it. "Why is that?" she asked as she sat back down.

Mrs. Tuttle, now standing at the door, folded her hands in front of her. "Creative people often have a harder time battling brain illnesses than those with no imagination."

Both women eyed her, waiting for her to continue.

The caregiver bowed her head and shook it. "The way this disease affects creative people has a certain cruelty to it. When two unconnected memories merge in an unimaginative person, that person realizes the combination

14

doesn't make sense. This makes them aware that something's wrong. Creative people on the other hand, simply create a plausible link between the two unrelated memories. They don't realize their new world doesn't exist and so they wait longer before seeking treatment. This morning your father said he dreamed of talking with two angels. I do my best to keep him grounded but he views my attempts as hostile, which, of course they're not."

With nothing further to add, Mrs. Tuttle, Anne and Eleanor exchanged good-byes and the care-giver left.

Eleanor then unfurled the folded cloth which turned out to be a large bib featuring a cartoon lobster with a handlebar mustache holding a glass of wine. As Eleanor tied it on, Anne put down her fork and scoffed with a dismissive shake of her head.

"What's your problem?" Eleanor asked as she reached for the bowl of spaghetti, filled her plate, took her fork, dug in and began twirling the spaghetti strands onto it.

Anne scowled. "Aren't you a little too old to be wearing a bib at the dinner table?"

Eleanor smirked. "I'm thirty-one. You can stop with the scolding mother bit. This blouse cost one hundred and twenty-five dollars. I don't want tomato sauce stains on it."

Anne shook her head and resumed eating.

An extended period of silence ensued. The only sounds were that of the ticking kitchen clock and silverware against the plate. Finally Anne wiped her mouth with her napkin and said "Could Mrs. Tuttle be right? Is Dad approaching the final phase?"

Spotting tiny drops of sauce on her bib, Eleanor grabbed the napkin and quickly wiped them off. As she

15

looked up, her lips pursed. "Sooner or later, Anne, it's going to happen. Dad's going to forget who we are, and no matter how many times we remind him, it's not going to make a difference. When that time comes, we'll put him in a nursing home or hospice, and that'll be that."

As Eleanor resumed eating, Anne leaned in. "How can you be so matter-of-fact about this?" she said pressing her hands on the table. "This is Dad we're talking about. Our dad. Our rock. Just the thought of him coming to his senses in some hospice and thinking we abandoned him…"

Eleanor looked up as she sucked some errant spaghetti strands into her mouth, chewed, swallowed and wiped her lips with her napkin. "Remember that story Dad told us about how *his* father died?" she asked.

Anne leaned back with a puzzled expression. "I don't remember him saying anything about his father's death, other than mentioning he'd been sick a lot."

Elle picked up a roll and began buttering it. "Oh, that's right. You were away training at the academy. Anyway, when Grandpa was dying, Dad visited him at the hospital every day after work. Uncle Dan was too upset by Grandpa's lingering illness, so he rarely visited, and when he did, it was only for a few minutes.

"This went on for months. And as Grandpa went downhill and the disease progressed, one day he started chewing Dad out for not visiting. 'Your brother Dan comes to see me every day," he told Dad. 'I'm lucky if you stop by once a month! Since it's too much of an infringement on your valuable time, don't bother coming back!"

"When Dad protested and tried to convince Grandpa that *he* was the one who visited every day, Grandpa called

16

him a G-D liar and told him he never wanted to see him again."

Anne was stunned and put down her fork. "At the end, Grandpa actually thought it was Uncle Dan who visited every day and not Dad?"

Eleanor nodded. "And apparently Grandpa kept his promise. Had Dad removed from the visitor list and he never saw his father again."

"Why didn't Grandma…"

"Dad said it wouldn't have mattered." Eleanor replied as she took a sip of wine. "Said at that stage his father's body was so toxic he didn't know what he was saying. Plus, the doctors were concerned about Grandpa's heart and told Dad if he continued to visit it might worsen his father's condition."

Anne shook her head, picked up her fork and resumed eating. "That is such a sad story."

Eleanor nodded and took a sip of wine. "My point is we can't worry about what Dad may think. With his mental deterioration, he might think the nursing home is a wonderland and his house a jail cell. We just need to do what has to be done."

Anne reluctantly nodded as she gazed into the living room and the fireplace mantle. In the center, amid various artwork and knick-knacks was a framed photo of their late younger brother Bob. Bob had passed away some years ago, before the onset of their father's illness. Both women suspected their brother's death may have triggered the virus that so ravaged their father's brain.

"It's times like these that I really miss Bob," Anne said wistfully as she picked up her wine glass. "Him with his, Don't-worry, everything-is-going-to-be-all-right, attitude.

17

The funny thing is whenever he said it, you actually believed it."

Eleanor smiled, then chuckled.

"What's so funny?"

Eleanor took a quick sip of her wine and said. "Remember our last Christmas dinner together? The one before Bob got sick? We were all sitting at this table reminiscing when Dad, after one too many glasses of Christmas cheer, starts getting all maudlin. Remember him putting his hand on Bob's shoulder and saying, 'Bob, if I ever get ill like my old man, I want you to take my pistol, place a pillow over my face and fire two shots into my head?'"

Anne burst out laughing, "Holy crap! Of course I remember that! And especially Dad's expression when Bob said, 'Hold that thought,' got up, went into the living room, came back with a pillow in his hand, pointed to his watch and said, 'You know, Dad, since I'm already here and have a little time to kill...'"

Eleanor's head snapped back as she roared with laughter. "To this day, it still cracks me up. Oh! And do you remember that affirmation Bob used to say to himself in the mirror just before he set out for work?

"Hold, hold," Anne said with a huge grin. "Let me see if I can." She pressed her hands to her temples, chuckled and said:

Mirrors, mirrors on the walls
Who's the guy with thee most balls?
Tis thee, my friend, you know it's true
Quote the raven
Yabba-dabba-do!

Eleanor laughed uproariously as her hand slapped the tabletop. "Geez, he was so much fun! I really miss him,"

18

she said between chuckles as she wiped the tears of laughter from her eyes.

"Me, too," Anne replied. Moments later, however, her expression turned thoughtful. "You know, I don't care what Mrs. Tuttle says, Elle. Dad's no lost cause. After we finish eating, let's go out in the back and see how he's doing."

Chapter 4

After I reluctantly finished a hearty meal of what looked like mealworms in bilge water, little Bosco O'Bama the Third and I walked along the wagon path on our way to the stables. There we would grab our horses and rifles for our trek into the Land o' Jungles section of Whateverland. As I unlocked the lock and pulled open the stable door, the boy asked, "Gam'pa, what does Mother mean when she warns you not fill my head with your loony-toon crap?"

As we entered and made our way inside, past the horses and toward the gun racks, I pondered his question. I pulled two AK-47's from the rack, handed one to Bosco, donned my pith helmet, handed a smaller version to him then replied, "Well, it's like this. Your mother, being a certified imbecile, has difficulty grasping life's complexities like chewing with her mouth closed or finding her ass with both hands, but to answer your question, and as I have explained to her on several occasions, there are complex problems in this world that cannot be resolved with simple solutions."

"Elucidate please, and with examples," he said, snapping in the magazine and checking the gun sight.

"I'll explain once we're out in the jungle," I replied. After swinging our rifles over our shoulders, opening the stalls, and saddling our horses, (Bosco's was actually a pony due to his smaller size) we rode out and into the vast acreage of the Land o' Jungles.

It was a beautiful late afternoon, the sun high and hot, the clouds, thin streams of vapor that scratched the sky. The tall grass swayed lazily in the breeze and the cicadas trilled their late-summer song as we clippity-clopped along.

"Bosco," I began, "many of today's problems are the result of not addressing the original concern when it first emerged. Take gun control. This country, since its inception, has permitted its citizens to own guns. As many as they want and mostly any type they want. The idea was to make sure the people could defend themselves should the government become evil and try to enslave them."

"Seems like a reasonable concept," Bosco O'Bama the Third said as we rode side-by-side though the tall grass.

"I agree. However, since that document was written, our armament technology has progressed in leaps and bounds. Back then, it took about a full minute to load and fire a rifle. An actual discharge occurred in, at best, three out of five attempts. Plenty of time for cooler heads to prevail. Today, we can wipe out an entire civilization in milliseconds with a device smaller than a suitcase."

Bosco nodded solemnly, "I can see where this may present a problem. Have you devised a solution?"

"Need you ask?" I replied smugly.

"I suppose not. Mother always says there isn't a blithering idiot on this planet who doesn't think he has the answer to all of mankind's woes."

"So true. All my blithering idiot friends think they're geniuses," I said, reminiscing. "Anyway, let's first address the possible solutions. One popular idea is to make owning a firearm illegal and force everyone to turn theirs in, the premise being that no guns means no murders."

"But there were murders long before guns were invented."

"Very true," I replied, swatting at an annoying fly. "Plus, there are 450 million guns in the United States and

21

the people who own them aren't going to voluntarily turn them over, meaning the government would have to use force, which would result in more people buying more guns to prevent their guns from being taken, which would result in tens of thousands of gun-related deaths instead of the piddly 9,000 we have every year."

"My, that's quite a dilemma," Bosco said striking a thoughtful pose. "Then what would be an intelligent and rational solution? And why on Earth am I asking you?"

"You're asking me because you want to know the answer. Well, there is no answer. There is no solution. The issue is too complex to be resolved without force, but using force will only *increase* the number of gun deaths, which the use of force was supposed to *decrease*!"

"So what do you suggest we do?" the boy asked.

"Execute anyone who offers a solution," I replied. "They're either stupid or crazy, and as such, too dangerous to be walking our streets."

Bosco gave me an odd sideways glance and was about to speak when…

"Ahoy and greetings, mateys," a voice called out from behind. I turned to see a man with a parrot on his shoulder approaching.

Pleasantly surprised, I smiled, stopped my horse and said, "Well, ahoy yourself, you old scallywag."

He was a big man with flowing white hair and a short white beard. He wore a white three-piece suit and peeking out from the pocket in his vest was a gold timepiece. He smiled as Bosco sidled up beside me and asked, "And who is this strapping young fella you got wit'cha?"

I turned to my grandson, gestured to the Cap'n and said, "Son, I'd like to introduce Cap'n Tom Spaulding, the African explorer."

"Hooray, hooray, hooray!" Bosco said. He studied the Cap'n with a bemused look.

Placing my hand on my grandson's shoulder, I looked at the Cap'n and said, "And this handsome young fella is Turtledove's boy, Bosco O'Bama the Third."

Cap'n Spaulding thrust out his hand. "It's a pleasure to meet you, lad. And I'd like to introduce my companion," he said pointing his thumb to the parrot on his shoulders. "His name is Polly. He learned to talk by listening to teenagers, and so speaks mostly in acronyms. Now I have a hard time figuring out what he's saying sometimes, but you young folks understand that stuff, right, ROFL?"

The red and green bird extended his head forward, stared eye to eye with the Cap'n and said "WTF?"

Cap'n Spaulding responded with a confused look then turned to me. "So what brings you to the Land o' Jungles?"

"Need to check on the animals," I replied as I lifted my binoculars from my chest and surveyed the landscape. "Caught Gladys in the trees again."

"Aye, she's a scamp, that one," the Cap'n noted as he quickly pulled and read his pocket watch. "But once done, how about we go for a sail? It's a beautiful day for it."

I looked around. It was indeed a beautiful day, and as I was about to accept the good Cap'n's offer, Bosco took my hand and pulled me to the side for a one-on-one palaver.

"Don't go with him," Bosco warned in a low tone. "There is something about him that is insidiously familiar."

That gave me pause. I've known the Cap'n for a while, and he's never given me reason to mistrust him, but Bosco

23

has powers and abilities far beyond those of mortal men, so when he speaks, I pay attention.

I heeded my grandson's warning and told the Cap'n I'd take a rain check. The Cap'n replied in good humor, "Some other time?"

When I nodded, he said, "Good day then, my fine fellows." And as he ambled down the path, Polly the parrot turned and said "TTYL."

After quick wave goodbye, Bosco and I continued on our journey.

Chapter 5

Later that evening, Anne peeked through the blinds into the back yard and said. "What in blazes is he doing out there?" She was watching her father talk to someone who wasn't there.

"Why? What's he up to now?" Eleanor asked as she came up alongside.

Anne rolled her eyes. "See for yourself. Geez!"

When Eleanor peeked through the slats, she burst out laughing. "Holy shit!" she giggled. "That's new! Look at him! He skipping around out there like those guys from *Monty Python and the Holy Grail* when they were pretending to be riding horses."

Anne shook her head and stepped from the window. "He looks ridiculous!"

Eleanor was still laughing. "All he needs now is some guy following him banging coconut halves together!"

"Mrs. Tuttle's right," Anne said in a huff. "He's clearly losing it."

"We don't know that," Eleanor replied, her laughter petering out. "Besides, he looks terrific. Seriously, look at him, He's sixty-five years old, still six-foot-two, still has all his hair which, let me point out is only slightly gray, has only minimum wrinkles, and frankly could be taken for a man in his late forties, early fifties. If he hadn't gotten sick, he'd be quite the catch." She released the slats and stepped from the window. "To me, it looks like he's having fun."

"It looks like he's out of his mind!" Anne shot back with a scowl.

"Oh ease up will you!? Maybe he's just playing around. Dad could be quite a goof when he wanted to be.

25

Let's put the rest of the food away and go outside and ask him how he's doing."

Anne scoffed. "He's off on one of his excursions. What would be the point?"

Elle gave a small smile and shrugged. "I don't know, maybe he'll let us ride along."

"Ughh," Anne said as she began gathering the dishes.

*

Shortly afterward, the silver gates to the Land o' Jungles opened and two angels came through. I reined to a stop, as did Bosco and we dismounted. As I turned to excuse myself from my grandson, I noticed he was already amusing himself by running after the chipmunks and squirrels in the brush.

"How are you feeling?" the shorter angel asked, taking my hand. They were both smiling. There was something about these two that always calmed and comforted me, made me feel that everything was going to be all right.

I'm feeling just fine," I replied, gently tapping her hand. "I was considering going for a boat ride but…" I was going to say that Bosco warned me against it, but decided to finish the sentence with, …I changed my mind," not comfortable bringing Bosco's concerns to their attention.

"Are you eating well?" the taller angel asked.

I shrugged and released the shorter one's hand, "Out here the food is good. Not like that crap Turtledove feeds me."

The angels turned to each other, then me. "Wait," the shorter one said, "Turtledoves?" She turned to the taller angel, "Turtledoves? Are they even edible?"

The taller angel shook her head. "He probably means chicken. Small chickens, like Cornish game hens."

26

The shorter one nodded, apparently satisfied.

I had no idea what they were referring to and was about to say so when I noticed that Bosco O'Bama the Third and his horse were gone! "Bosco!" I called out as I quickly scanned the area. "Bosco!"

I became concerned. The Land o' Jungles can be a dangerous place, particularly if you get lost. With no time to lose, I immediately mounted my steed, unshouldered my rifle, and rode off.

"Where are you going?" the tall one called out.

I had no time for foolish questions. "Where does it look like?" I snapped, spurring my steed. "I have to get Bosco!" I shouted as I tore through the high brush. "Bosco!"

The angels followed but soon fell behind.

I needed to cover as much ground as possible. The sun was going down and my concerns for Bosco's well-being were growing. I continued calling his name as my steed and I dashed across the fields, but there was no reply.

As the sun disappeared behind the horizon and the lands grew dark, a solid shaft of pure white light running from the ground to the clouds appeared in the distance.

Frightened, I stopped and shouted, "Bosco!"

Suddenly, I heard his voice. It was distant, about as far away as the beam of light. He said, "Don't worry about me, Gam'pa. I'm here. I'm always here. You never have to worry about me ever again."

The shaft of light slowly dimmed then went out. The moon's light now illuminated the vast fields of the Land o' Jungles. The trees became silhouettes, as did the distant hills. Clouds drifted, stars twinkled and a soft breeze blew through my hair as the world retired for the night.

27

"Here you go," the angels said as the tall one tapped me on the shoulder.

I was surprised they had caught up to me so quickly, but then remembered angels can fly, so I turned and said, "I'm sorry for being short-tempered earlier, but I was looking for Bosco."

She nodded. "We know," she said and handed me a cup of what smelled like hot chocolate. "We warmed it up figuring you would prefer it that way now that the weather's cooling down."

I was tired from all the activity and needed to rest. I announced to the vast fields of the Land o' Jungles that I was calling it a night and going back to the house. Bosco replied by saying that was fine and that he'd be along directly.

*

Early Monday morning, Anne knocked on Eleanor's door and after opening it said, "Rise and shine, lazy bones. Mrs. Tuttle will be here in an hour and I have to get a move on if I'm going to get to work on time." She was wearing a light blue bathrobe and had two towels folded over her forearm.

"All right, all right, you pain in the ass!" Eleanor growled, rising begrudgingly from the red and white sheets and blankets and then playfully flinging her pillow at her sister. "Is Dad up yet?"

"No," Anne replied as she easily caught the projectile. "I'm hoping he stays asleep until Mrs. Tuttle gets here. She's better at keeping him in line than we are. I'm going to take a shower. Give me ten minutes before you flush the toilet."

Eleanor nodded as Anne tossed the pillow back and closed the door. Sliding off the bed, she stepped into her slippers, took her robe from the bedpost and put it on. As she tied its red sash, she looked out the window into the pale blues and yellows of the morning sky.

How did my life get this nuts? she asked her reflection in the glass with a sigh. *Thirty-one years old and back in my old bedroom in my parents' house. I...*

Her reverie was interrupted by her cell phone ringing. She pulled it from her purse, saw who was calling and rolled her eyes. "What does this idiot want?" She clicked it on. "Yes, Elliot. What's up?"

A pause, then... "What? No, that's out of the question. I'm not coming in. I told you I was taking this week off to tend to my father." Another pause. "Well unforeseen circumstances or not I gave you ample time to make other arrangements. The Goldenrod Hotel will have to 'make do' without me this week."

Eleanor walked to her closet as she listened. "Oh don't give me that executive vice-presidents are always on call nonsense. You're the CEO, so grab someone from another project and have them handle it until I come back. What?!! You might want to rethink that, Elliot. I don't like veiled threats and if you push me too hard, I'll push back. Now I have to go, goodbye."

She ended the call, placed the phone in her robe and opened her closet door.

Probably not the best way to handle that. Especially with Elliot being such a mean-spirited bastard, but he knows how serious my situation is.

She shook her head in disgust. *Prick! If I didn't need this job right now...*

As she selected the clothes to wear that day, she recalled how her father had somehow managed to hold everything together after their mother secretly emptied the

29

family's joint savings account, as well as Eleanor's, Anne's and Bob's college funds and ran off with the owner of a micro-brewery.

As she gazed into the mirror on the back of the closet door and held the day's potential blouse to her chest, she also recalled how quickly things went from bad to worse moneywise. Those endless months of macaroni and cheese for dinner. Peanut butter and jelly sandwiches for lunch every day. Cheap generic cereal for breakfast. At one point their finances got so tight they almost lost the house. Fortunately, Dad found a second job and slowly, over time, he turned things around.

But in the end, it was Brainiac Bob, their kid brother, who catapulted the August family to financial success.

Always the prankster, he created a number of comically entertaining apps for Smartphones. After the family pooled their money to fund Bob's venture, they were pleasantly surprised when his start-up netted a tremendous profit on their relatively small investment. Within months he owned one of New York's most successful software businesess.

Over the following two years nearly everything they did brought positive results. They were all making good money at their jobs, bought new cars, went on vacations, had a new roof and siding put on the house—and it seemed the best was yet to come.

Life was good!

Then tragedy struck. As Bob's company grew, the demands on his time grew too. He often put in fifteen-hour days and rarely had a day off. Being only twenty-four, he didn't give much thought to health insurance. He had never been sick and had enough money socked away should some drawn out illness or bone breaking accident temporarily sideline him. But he was wrong.

So very wrong.

Eleanor wiped a tear from her eye with the heel of her hand, walked into her bathroom and took her morning tinkle. Once done, she looked up and said with an emotion-choked voice, "Rest in peace, Bob. Rest in peace."

As she shook her head and flushed the toilet, she heard her sister in the downstairs bathroom shower yell, "Owwwwwwwwww! Damn it, Eleanor!"

As the toilet water swirled, Eleanor grimaced and meekly called out, "Sorry, sis."

*

That morning, Turtledove kicked open my bedroom door, stormed in, yanked me up and said, "Get your clothes on, we're going for a ride". She said she had contracted the services of a woman who, in order to ease my memory lapses, would jab pins into me until I look like Pinhead from the movie *Hellraiser*. She said it's because she cares and will do whatever it takes to ease my suffering.

"Yeah, right," I said sarcastically as I watched her repeatedly slap her thick black billy club against her open palm.

"Just get dressed. I'll be back in two minutes, so you'd better be ready." With that, she turned and charged out the door.

Personally, I suspect she might be anxiously awaiting my demise so she can inherit the vast August family fortune. Won't she be surprised when she finds out I left it all to Bosco?!

With that happy thought in mind, I dressed and had just finished putting on my shoes when Turtledove flung open the door and said, "Let's go!"

Not one to be pushed around I said, "Wait just one damn minute! I'll go when I'm damn good and ready!" momentarily forgetting that Turtledove, like all August family women, is immensely powerful and Amazonian in physique.

She eyed me, laughed her evil laugh, then effortlessly picked me up, flung me over her shoulder, carried me outside, threw me into the trunk of her car, took me to this odd hippie place, hurled me into the room and said to the woman there, "Kill him or cure him, doc. I can't take another minute of this mush brain's yammering."

After my daughter left, I found myself lying helpless on this hippie woman's table. The place was like a clogged colon of colored scarfs, wind chimes and objects made out of yarn. The burning insense smelled like someone set fire to a pair of old gym socks.

The next thing I knew there was some oddball flute and seashore sounds playing in the background as she begins jamming pins into my head. She asked what my problem was and I said, "Some strange hippie woman is jamming pins in my head."

She laughed and replied, "It's being done to help you remember,"

So I said, "Who the hell is going to forget having pins jammed into their head?"

She laughed again.

Honestly, I failed to see the humor.

Just then, Admiral Akbar from *Star Wars/Return of the Jedi* burst in and yelled, "It's a trap!"

I knew it!

32

I leapt up and charged out of the room and into a drum circle or whatever you call the area where these like-minded lunatics congregate. Unfortunately, Turtledove saw me and before I could escape, she tackled and wrestled me to the floor. I shouted, "Hey, take it easy. I got pins in my head!"

She replied, "You're going to have my boot in your ass if you don't stop screwing around. Now get back in there and let the nice lady finish your treatment."

Facing her formidable strength and firepower, I reluctantly complied.

Shortly afterward, the hippie woman again left me to the cacophony of flutes and bongos and harps and the sound of falling rain which only made me want to pee. Finally, she returned and removed the pins. I had barely gotten my bearings when Turtledove bum-rushed me out, again threw me in the trunk and drove me to the Land of the Spacesuit People.

At this point, I'm going off the rails on a crazy train.

The next thing I knew, I was wearing this green linen shirt and pants and my feet are in cloth slippers. Then Turtledove dragged me into a room with a Dodge mini-van in the center. I had no freakin' idea what was going on. Then this woman wearing a huge smile laid me down on this white autopsy table and clamped a plastic milk-crate-type thing to it, which covered my chest and kept me from moving. Then she stuck plugs in my ears and slowly slid me under the mini-van. And if that wasn't bad enough, some guy came in with a bass drum and started pounding on it.

I admit I was starting to lose it and might have gone off the rails completely had not Bosco O'Bama the Third shown up. When I saw that familiar round head with its firetruck red hair, I breathed a sigh of relief. I was about to ask him to get me out of there, but he put his finger to his lips and said, "Shhhh." He kept hidden, looked around and added. "I can't let them see me or they'll make me leave, but I've been under one of those contraptions myself and there's no use struggling. Just close your eyes and count to 1,800. When you reach 1,800 the guy with the drum will leave and the lady will roll you out from under the mini-van. I'll explain everything later at Whateverland."

He again raised his finger to his lips, winked, said, "Shhhh" again and left.

Since Bosco O'Bama the Third is the smartest person I know, I took his advice and sure enough, just as I approached the number 1,800 the drum stopped and the lady returned, wheeled me out and removed the plastic crate that held me in place.

I slowly climbed to my feet.

Again with the big smile she took my arm to steady me and said, "Now, that wasn't so bad was..."

That's when I cocked my fist and swung. Unfortunately, Turtledove, anticipating my response, hip-checked me and sent me careening into the door.

As Turtledove grabbed my arm, dragged me outside and into the parking lot, I pulled free and shouted, "Hold on. We can't leave without Bosco O'Bama the Third. How's he going to get home?"

Turtledove stared at me, puzzled. "Who's Bosco O'Bama the Third?"

I stared back, astounded that this woman, the one insisting *I* had memory problems, didn't know who I was talking about. So I got right into her face. "He's your son, for heaven's sake!" I shook my head in disbelief. "You can't even remember your own son? How'd you like it if I

34

forgot who you were, huh? How'd you like that, Turtledove?"

She just stared at me, mumbled something under her breath, grabbed my arm and resumed dragging me to the car.

Chapter 6

When Anne and Eleanor arrived at their father's house that evening, they found Mrs. Tuttle slumped in the recliner in the darkened living room. The shades were open, although it was well past twilight. The sparsely furnished room was reminiscent of old black-and- white photographs, the ones from the Great Depression where faces were hard and lines deep.

Mrs. Tuttle had obviously been an attractive woman as her simple yet elegant features did attest, but the years and the rigors of her profession had chiseled away whatever softness and petite femininity she once carried and replaced them with sharp angles, thin lines and bitter resolve.

"Rough day, huh?" Eleanor said as she closed the blinds and pulled the curtains. As Anne flicked on the overhead light, color flooded the room, Mrs. Tuttle, with a forlorn expression, reached for her tea cup and took a sip. Placing the cup down, she eyed the two sisters coldly and said, "He's becoming violent."

Anne immediately paled, stopped and turned. "What'd he do?"

"He swung at the MRI technician. If I hadn't noticed his closed fist and pushed him off-balance, he'd a knocked her cold."

"He tried to punch one of the techs?" Eleanor asked with startled concern. She pulled a cigarette from her purse and immediately lit it.

Mrs. Tuttle's response was a quick nod.

"Geez," Anne said as she raised her hand to her forehead. "That is so unlike him." She huffed and looked up. "So how did the acupuncture go?"

36

Mrs. Tuttle rolled her eyes. "Fine until some wall-eyed guy, obviously lost, walked in on your father midway through his treatment. That spooked your dad and he charged out of the room hell-bent for leather. Fortunately, I was in the waiting room and caught him before he made it to the door."

"Thank you, Mrs. Tuttle," Eleanor said as she dropped onto the couch and placed her hand on the caregiver's forearm. "We can't thank you enough for taking such good care of Dad. If you had only met him before he got ill, you could see why Anne and I care so much. He was a wonderful father. It's so painful..." she bit her lower lip. "...to see him coming apart. And the thought of him turning violent. It's... it's just so unlike him."

"I can only imagine," Mrs. Tuttle replied, her face taut as she took another sip of tea. "But there was another incident today that troubled me."

Concerned, Eleanor leaned in. "And what was that?"

Mrs. Tuttle returned the teacup to its saucer and placed both on the end table. She leaned forward and with clasped hands said, "When we left the Imaging Center after his MRI, your father told me we needed to wait for, now get this, Bosco O'Bama the Third."

"Bosco O'Bama the Third?" Anne asked with a puzzled expression. "Who's that?"

Mrs. Tuttle rolled her eyes and shrugged. "Your father said he was my son! Then I think he called me Turtledove."

"Turtledove? Where do I know that from?" Eleanor asked Anne.

"From the other night," Anne replied. "Dad said he ate fine outside but not that crap Turtledove fed him."

37

"Why would he call Mrs. Tuttle, Turtledov..." Her face lit up, "Oh, he's re-associating words like that woman whose husband's name was Jim Beau. And what was that about your son?" Eleanor asked, taking a pull from her cigarette. "You don't have a son."

Mrs. Tuttle nodded. "That's right. And since I never had children, I didn't know how to respond. Then he admonished me for being forgetful and asked how'd I like it if he forgot who I was?"

"Wait!" Anne said running her hand through her long hair. "Are we sure he even knows who you are?"

Mrs. Tuttle again shrugged her shoulders, followed by an I-haven't-a-clue expression.

As Anne stepped forward to press for answers, Eleanor stood and said. "What were the results of the MRI?"

"The preliminary medical report is over there," she replied with a tilt of her head to the hardwood table next to the front door. "It'll take days before we have the complete test results, but it isn't looking good. Judging by his actions, the meds are having little effect on the deterioration and seemingly no effect at all regarding the confusion and forgetfulness."

"What's he doing now?" Anne asked as she walked to the table to have a look at the reports.

Mrs. Tuttle replied, "He's sitting in his bedroom staring out the window, holding lengthy conversations with people who aren't there."

*

I awoke in the middle of the night, something I rarely do. Probably because of the meds I take, or should I say Turtledove forces me to take. There was a light in the window. Curious, I got up and went for a look. It seemed

38

cold in the room, but the thermostat read 68 degrees, so maybe it's me.

When I reached the window, I noticed it was that same shaft of pure white light I saw in the Land o' Jungles the other evening while searching for Bosco O'Bama the Third. I'm so glad he told me he was all right. I get so worried sometimes.

I shivered as the cold embraced me, vapor billowing from my mouth as I breathed, but I couldn't stop staring at that light. There's something wrong about it. Something that says it shouldn't be there... something...

I jerked back, startled. Apparently I had been staring at it for quite some time. Tears were rolling down my face.

What brought that on?

I returned my attention to the beam and felt an emptiness in the pit of my stomach, a feeling of profound loss.

Could Turtledove be right? Is there truly something wrong with me?

I abandoned the window, settled into bed and sang my nightly prayer.

Be-fore I slip into- unconsciousness, I'd- like to have a-nother kiss, another-flashing –chance-at bliss. A-nother kiss, a-nother kiss. AMEN

Chapter 7

"Gam'pa! Gam'pa!" Bosco shouted excitedly as he burst into my bedroom the following morning. "It's time to get up and play!" He leapt on top of the bed and jumped up and down.

Rustling my way from under the blankets, I shook my head and tried to clear my thoughts. I waved for Bosco to stop jumping. "Okay, okay, you little scamp," I said slowly sitting up and tousling the boy's hair as he jumped down. "But first, I'll need a little privacy to get dressed and say my morning prayers."

"Morning prayers?" he said with a curious expression. "Isn't prayer an antiquated religious rite?"

"Not at all. I use it to keep in touch with my Maker," I said as I stepped into my slippers.

Bosco sat down beside me. "Mother said I was made in the backseat of a Greyhound bus rolling down Highway 41."

"I have no doubt," I said, shaking my head disapprovingly.

"We don't have religious rituals at our house," Bosco added. "Mother says religion is a collection of silly stories made up by crazy people who believe there is an invisible man in the sky who loves you and wants nothing more than for you to be happy."

"Well, if that God exists, I'd sure like to meet Him because the God I know is nothing like that. The God I know scares the shit out of me!"

"Really? Wow, Gam'pa!" Bosco beamed with surprise. "I wonder why Mother never told me about your religious beliefs."

"Probably because, although your dear mother grew up in this very house, she doesn't subscribe to the tenets of my faith."

"Please elaborate," little Bosco said as he folded his hands in his lap.

Geez. I do so love this kid! With his big, innocent eyes and gapped-tooth smile.

"Well," I began, "my beliefs fall outside normal parameters. Most people believe God created them and placed them on Earth to lead good and productive lives. Others believe that if you do wrong in this life, you're sent back to make up for it. There are many, many different beliefs, but I don't buy into any of them because I've already figured out why I'm here."

Overhearing this, my beloved daughter Turtledove stormed in and bellowed, "Don't you go filling my son's head with that loony-toon crap, you insane old douchebag!"

"Mother, please!" Bosco says, grabbing my arm to keep me from flinging my alarm clock at her. "We need to respect all religions as long as they don't promote violence or hatred, no matter how stupid or asinine. And we should especially respect those of people like Gam'pa, who, as we know, could snap and go on a killing spree at any moment."

My daughter nodded solemnly. "As usual, you're right, and all I ask, my son, is that you let whatever he says go in one ear and out the other."

"Don't I always, Mother?" he replied.

After she left, Bosco winked at me and I continued my tale.

"So here's what happened. I'm originally from another planet or dimension or alternative reality or whatever—

41

just some other place. And in that place, everyone is like me. They can all write books and music and draw and tell jokes and basically entertain each other without needing television or movies. And because we're all happy doing that, there are never any wars or riots or social unrest because it would take away from our creative time, and we're all simply too busy to muck about with such nonsense.

"Well, *almost* all of us.

"You see, Bosco, in the middle of all this joy, all this fun, one damned fool decided it wasn't enough to be happy and fulfilled. No! He wanted to be a ruler; a king. He wanted all the attention focused on him and for everybody to do what he told them. And so he set out and made this seriously stupid idea a reality, which made everybody very unhappy for a long time.

"Fortunately, one day, God happened to be driving by in His Mercedes Benz, and yes, being God, He undoubtedly values German engineering. When He saw what had occurred, He pulled a Glock 9 and shot that jerk in the ass."

"And all the people lived happily ever after!" Bosco said with a big smile.

"They sure did," I said, patting him on the knee. "But the story isn't over. You see, the guy who made everybody miserable had to appear before God to explain why. Of course he couldn't, so God said, "Since you like making people miserable, I'm going to send you to a place where they specialize in it."

Bosco eyed me. "Am I to assume that you're the dick who made everybody miserable and as punishment got sent to Earth?"

"Apparently so," I replied. "And boy, was God right about the people here. I mean, what's wrong with them? Have you read the history of this place? Do you have any idea what these lunatics regularly do to each other? Seriously, who came up with the idea of nailing somebody to a cross? And why, when that psycho suggested it, didn't everybody grab him and put him in a mental institution? Same goes for burning people at the stake. Holy cannoli, Bosco! They set human beings on fire because they believed these people weren't really human beings but imaginary characters known as witches. That would be like a mob dragging me off to hang me because they believed I was a Klingon."

"I'd join that mob," Turtledove called out from the hallway.

I ignored her and shook my head. "It's not like we don't know better. The great philosophers of the ages all promoted peace. Aristotle, Confucius, Gandhi and especially Rodney King, whose immortal words, 'Can't we all just get along?' have become the lynchpin of my belief system."

Bosco O'Bama the Third rose and headed for the door. "I'll leave you to your morning rituals. And when you speak to this God of yours, request that He stop pummeling you. I don't like seeing my Gam'pa hurt."

43

Chapter 8

It was raining heavily the following Monday as Anne and Eleanor sat at the kitchen table drinking coffee. The sky was dark and matted with thick grey clouds. An occasional burst of thunder echoed following a flash of light that momentarily lit the room.

They were waiting for Mrs. Tuttle to arrive. Anne in a dark blue pants suit and Eleanor in light gray. Both were impatient to leave for work.

Eleanor lit a cigarette and Anne snarled and waved her hand to dispel the smoke that didn't exist yet.

Spending the last week full-time at their father's house had proved a real inconvenience. The increasing pressure brought about by their father's illness and deterioration had raised tensions and shortened tempers. Plus, there hadn't been any noticeable changes to the house's interior since they lived there as children and the old ghosts of those hard times continued to haunt them. The black burn mark on the table, created by their mother's cigarette many years ago following a drunken argument with their father. The tea kettle she had thrown at him was still on the stove. The square digital clock that had been set to chime when it was time for their brother Bob to take his meds still stood above the kitchen sink. One reminder after another of past difficulties.

Anne pursed her lips tightly when she eyed the dog dish peeking out from the bottom of the slightly ajar pot and pan cupboard next to the stove. A dish for a dog dead these past eleven years.

The place had become the Ghost of Christmas Past in and of itself.

As rainwater streaked the window panes and pecked the skylight, Eleanor, in the dim glow of the overhead light placed her coffee cup on the saucer, looked up and said, "When the time comes to commit Dad, what are we going to do with his stuff?"

Anne sat back and rubbed the remaining sleep out of her eyes. "Oh, I don't know," she said stifling a yawn. "We can easily sell his musical instruments. He took good care of them."

Eleanor shrugged. "Yeah, but it's not like they're collector's items. From what I can see, they're cheap knock-offs made to look like name brands. I suppose Mom might like them. I can ask."

Anne suddenly bolted forward, her face reddening. "Wait! You've been talking to Mom?!"

Eleanor sighed and rolled her eyes, instantly regretting mentioning their mother, a topic that always enraged her sister. "Let it go, will you? It's been over twenty-years since she abandoned us. I'm not going to hold a grudge for the rest of my life. Regardless of what she's done, she's still our mother."

"Fuck… her!" Anne spat as she accidently kicked the table leg causing the coffee cups to jostle and spill a little into the saucers. Eleanor recoiled as Anne suddenly leapt to her feet and wagged her finger accusingly at her. "I'll never speak to that bitch for as long as I live. And she's not getting his instruments. I'll burn the fucking things before I let her have them."

Eleanor leaned back and raised her hands. "Will you please calm down? You're acting like a freakin' lunatic. Look, I get why you're pissed. You got stuck taking care of me and Bob after Mom left, which was no small task but, remember, Mom and Dad were bohemians and made

45

no bones about their past." Eleanor shrugged. "You've got to face facts, hon. Rock n' rollers are not the most stable of people."

Anne grimaced as she dropped back into her chair and folded her arms. "I meant what I said, she's not getting any of his stuff."

"Fine!" Eleanor said as she took a drag, then got up and looked around for an ashtray. She was about to give up and use the saucer when she noticed one of those small Table Talk aluminum pie plates sticking out of the metal trashcan. She grabbed it, bent a small lip on its edge to hold her cigarette, then sat back down.

Satisfied, she tapped the cigarette in the makeshift ashtray. "I won't mention the instruments to Mom. I'll sell them on eBay or something." She turned to the window to look for any sign of Mrs. Tuttle. "You know, I've often wondered why Mom and Dad didn't make it to the big time. They were certainly talented enough. I'm amazed each time I listen to that tape of their songs. All those shitty bands got record contracts back then, while really great bands like Mom and Dad's never got a break."

With a puzzled look, Anne tilted her head and leaned forward. "You have a tape of the songs Mom and Dad recorded? I thought all their tapes and videos were destroyed when their studio burned down."

"They were, except for the one I got," Eleanor replied, taking another drag as she eyed the digital clock. *Beat cheeks, Tuttle, damn it! It's my first day back to work and I don't want to be late and have to deal with that prick Elliot.*

"Anyway," Eleanor continued, "one afternoon after school I found Mom writing a piano overdub for one of their songs. It was really good, so I asked her to make a tape of all their tunes so I could listen to it on the way to school. She did, and I kept it in my locker. After the fire I told her I still had the tape, but she didn't seem to care. Looking back, I think that might have been the beginning of the end for Mom and Dad."

Anne sneered and waved dismissively. "Her fucking that beer bum was the end for Mom and Dad."

"Keep in mind who we're talking about," Eleanor said as she leaned back, crossed her legs and blew a cloud of smoke into the air. "The fire destroyed **everything** they spent their lives creating."

She had drawn out the word 'everything' to add emphasis.

Anne wasn't buying. "So what? A lot of people rebuild after stuff burns down. She wasn't the first person that happened to, you know."

Eleanor tapped the ash. "True, but I think Mom saw it as a sign. A sign that the music thing wasn't going to work out. Think about it. They were already in their thirties, we were approaching our teens, and Mom may have been a lot of things but a hausfrau was never one of them. So, faced with the choice of living out the rest of her life in a dreary, middle-class environment or running away with a rich, micro-brewery owner, she chose the latter. Don't know if I'd do any different."

"You'd steal the family's money and abandoned your own son and daughters?" Anne asked with a wry look.

Eleanor bit down and with a snarl, crushed out her cigarette. "Where the hell is Mrs. Tuttle?"

Just then the front door opened and Mrs. Tuttle entered, dressed in a black trench coat and gray plastic hat. She backed into the room as she closed her umbrella and shook it out before closing the door. After she placed it in

47

the umbrella stand, she removed her coat and said, "Pretty nasty out there. Be careful driving to work. I saw two accidents on the way in."

*

Following one of Turtledove's horrible dinners of gristle and something that tasted like tar balls, I decided to go for an evening stroll. I left the house and casually strolled to the gates of the Land o' the Future. As I was about to enter, Bosco O'Bama the Third called out, "Wait for me!"

As he came alongside, Bosco took my hand and said, "How come you left without me? You know how much I enjoy spending time with you in Whateverland."

I gave a solemn nod. "I know, but Land o' the Future is really not a place for children. Too dangerous."

Bosco carefully studied the landscape, then with a puzzled expression asked, "Even more so than Land o' Jungles?"

I nodded. "If you have a gun you can deal with whatever is happening in the Land o' Jungles. That's not always true in Land o' the Future."

As we walked through the gates the boy asked, "Why?"

I took a moment to come up with the best answer I could think of. "In the Land O' the Future you can often see what's going to happen but you can't do anything about it."

Bosco titled his head. "But if it's a good thing why would you WANT to do anything about it, Pop-Pop?"

I stopped dead in my tracks, stunned that he had called me 'Pop-Pop'. It was then I noticed the boy looked noticeably different. He had dark coloring around his left eye and there were several bruises on his arms. "What

48

happened to you? Get in a fight?" I asked as I scooched down for a better look.

Bosco lowered his head and nodded. "Yeah," he said solemnly.

Well, boys will be boys, I thought. I patted him on the shoulder and said, "Well, I'll wager he looks a lot worse than you do." I was hoping that would generate a smile but instead the boy turned pensive.

"Unfortunately not," Bosco O'Bama the Third replied. "He's surprisingly agile. I came right at him but couldn't lay a hand on him. He kept landing shots. Slipped all my punches. Anyway, my friends are going to teach me how to fight him. He won't be so lucky the next time we go at it."

"That's the right attitude," I said trying to be supportive, though those marks and bruises concerned me. "You get a couple of good shots in and he'll leave you alone, you'll see."

That seemed to help and the boy lost that troubled look.

"So what's this kid's name?"

Bosco eyed the ground again. "Luke. I never saw this kid in school before, but my friends said he's always getting into fights. They said he's gotten his ass kicked more than once, so..."

I shook my head and exhaled. "Unfortunately, I know the type. Kids from broken homes, filled with rage because they feel they got the short end of the stick. They lash out at anyone they think will take it. Next time, give him a shot straight in the breadbasket," I said, patting my midsection. "That'll slow him down. And when he's bent over, give him a sock on the jaw. It's the law of the jungle, my boy. The predators always prey on the ones they view as defenseless. You show this predator you're no easy mark."

There was something else about Bosco, though, that seemed off-kilter.

I leaned in for a closer look. "How old are you now?"

"I'm nine."

"Hmmm," I said as I took his hand.

Not much more was said as we walked and took in the surroundings.

With a backdrop of long pillows of red clouds on a light gray sky, lines of ten-feet tall holographic computer code whistled by like a high-speed bullettrain. Tall, white cement poles extended in a straight line as far as the eye could see. Crooked fingers of electricity crackled from its tips as it danced from pole to pole. And to the right was an aquamarine body of water laden with thousands of wind turbines that cast spotlights across the water. Everything, it appeared, was built to grab your attention, to engage your curiosity, to pique your interest.

As we strolled I said, "The problem with Land o' the Future is that it's all show and no substance. All flash and pizazz. It's a testament to Man's inability to create anything that lasts."

Approaching the shoreline of the slowly lapping aquamarine waters, we saw an ornate castle upon a rock, high above and constructed of black marble. The top had many tall spires, each of which had several objects similar to bass drums attached to them. It towered over the waters and reflected the sun's rays like a finely cut diamond. A fortress clearly created to withstand the ravages of time.

Bosco looked up and said, "But Pop-Pop, some things do last. Look at the pyramids. They've been around for thousands of years."

I smiled and patted his shoulder as we walked. "Funny you should choose that example. The pyramids, some of the oldest structures in recorded history, are actually mausoleums. Grave markers of a bygone people and a building technology that has been lost to the ages. Sooner or later everything is lost, leaving their skeletons to be mistakenly viewed as monuments."

Bosco shook his head. "I respectfully disagree. It isn't the things themselves that are important, it's what they represent. The pyramids aren't merely mausoleums, they're a symbol, a reminder that the impossible can be accomplished. The national parks aren't just campgrounds, they are a gift from our ancestors and a legacy that reminds us of the importance of preserving nature's beauty. And it's the crucifix that reminds us that even after two thousand years the words of a simple carpenter still resonate and remind mankind to resist its violent tendencies and base urges, and to instead love all those we've been imprisoned with, because we're all being punished. And being punished hurts."

I was taken aback and said. "You sure you're only nine? I swear, Bosco O'Bama the Third, you never cease to amaze me!"

A strong wind suddenly struck and nearly knocked Bosco off his feet. I anchored myself with a firm stance and stood over the boy, providing shelter as best I could.

It was then, as I turned toward the castle, that I saw it was made of sand. It's deceivingly powerful edifice scattered wildly and disappeared into the red clouds above. Minutes later, as the winds died down, it was almost completely gone.

Stunned Bosco stared at the once massive structure. "It's… it's..." He was unable to find the words.

"It's all right," I said, taking the boy's hand. "Everything that disappears does so to make room for what is to follow. Each generation has its own particular needs, joys and sorrows. Everything is created for a specific purpose, and to last for a specific time. Every so often I'll play some of the songs I wrote and remember how good they were when I created them. But now time is wearing away their brilliance, their magic. With the birth of each new song, my songs age and deteriorate and eventually will be forgotten. Nothing is permanent."

Bosco O'Bama the Third smiled. "Maybe not permanent in form, but they resonate in spirit. Nothing really disappears. Every song begins a path for others to follow. Every painting, every novel, everything we do, has a ripple effect that spans the centuries."

As the boy spoke, the winds returned as powerful as ever. And again I became a bastion, protecting Bosco from the gale forces. When they finally subsided, and as I brushed at my clothes, Bosco, eyes wide with wonder, said, "Look, Pop-Pop!" And as I followed the boy's pointed finger, I saw the castle had been rebuilt. It was not exactly the same castle. It was different in style and design, but very much the same in size.

We continued walking until we reached the pier. Jutting deep into the aquamarine waters, a boat was docking. From the deck of the craft a man in white waved.

It was Cap'n Spaulding.

Bosco tugged on my arm indicating he wanted to keep going, but I said to do so without returning the greeting would be rude. So we waited until he completed tying his boat to the dock. Shortly afterward he joined us on shore.

"Greeting and salutations, my friends," the Cap'n said as he approached with his hand extended.

As I shook it, Polly the parrot tilted his head and said, "Sup?"

"We're just enjoying a brief stroll," Bosco O'Bama the Third said, tightening his grip on my hand.

I knew what he was trying to convey. Apparently the boy's suspicions about the good Cap'n had not been assuaged.

"Beautiful evening for a sail," the Cap'n said, spreading his hand toward the aquamarine waters and the purple sun resting on the horizon.

Just then one of the angels appeared and said, "Dad, come quick, Anne's in the hospital. She's been shot!"

Chapter 9

My arms flew from my sides. I was falling, falling, falllllliiiinnnnnnnng…

Anne?

And there she was, her adorable little round three-year-old face, her sparkling green eyes, her dimpled smile, holding my hand and her mother's as we walked down our street.

"Q,R,S,T,U,V,W" she sang… "X,Y,Z. Now I know my ABCs, next time won't you sing with me?" That darling little face, with all its love and childhood joy, looked up at me and her mother and asked, "Would you like to sing with me, buddies?"

Anne?

And we sang. We sang those ABCs together, all three of us. And God saw it was good.

Anne?

"Dad, did you hear me? Anne's been shot!"

And then there she was in her playpen, three years old, vomiting every fifteen minutes. All through the night. The flu ravaged my sparkling little girl. And all I could do was sit in a chair alongside, making the bucket available when needed. Useless. I was just… useless.

After one horrific bout of vomiting followed by several painful dry heaves, that pretty little face, with its sparkling green eyes filled with tears, reached over, took my hand and in a shaky, frightened voice said, "Daddy, help me." She reached out her arms.

"Daddy, please help me."

54

I swept her into my arms, careful not to squeeze her, careful to protect her. Ready to charge into hell itself if that's what it took, if that's what it took to save her.

But I was helpless, useless. There was nothing I could do. And I *saw* that horrifying realization in her eyes when she began vomiting yet again.

Finally, after what seemed an eternity, she fell asleep in my arms. I held her straight through till morning. I would be holding her still if that's what it took.

But come morning the fever broke. And when my wife arrived home from work, she changed the sheets, cleaned the mess, and convinced me to lay her down on the fresh, cool linens of her newly made bed. And as I lay her down her eyes opened dreamily and she said, "I love you, Daddy. You make me feel safe."

But I hadn't. I had been useless.

Anne's been shot?

"ANNE!!" I shouted and the world blew away.

Eleanor's father suddenly found himself standing in his back yard. He quickly looked around having no idea how he got there.

What time is it? What day is it? he wondered.

Then he realized there were more important matters to deal with.

He grabbed Eleanor by the shoulders and said, "Anne's been shot?"

Tearfully, Eleanor nodded.

"How bad is it?" he asked.

With eyes wide with panic, she started shaking. "I don't know. I don't know!" she exclaimed almost hysterically. She clasped her hands to the side of her head and began pacing. "They just called and said she was

55

taken to Albany Med. Said two guys carjacked a family van and were using the kids as hostages. They shot the father. Anne was nearby on the highway when she heard the call on the police scanner, so she rushed over. And that's when they shot her. I... I..."

Her emotions overwhelmed her and she began sobbing uncontrollably.

He pulled her in, hugged her tight and steadied her. Then whispered. "Remember what I told you about these situations?"

She pulled away, clearly stunned. She eyed him angrily, and he eyed her right back. Moments later the crying stopped. She dipped into her pocket for a tissue, wiped her eyes and nose, then said in a choked, trembling voice, "A crying person is a... useless person. Solve the problem first... then cry all you want."

She sniffed a few times and paused for a moment. "You're right, you're absolutely right. Here I am blubbering like a child when my sister is in the hospital and may need a transfusion."

He started searching his pockets for his car keys. Then his cell phone, figuring he'd call the hospital and get an update on her condition.

He was startled to find his pockets empty. There was nothing in them. Nothing at all. Not even his wallet which he ALWAYS carried because it contained his cards, money, and licenses.

As he tried to figure out why they were missing, Eleanor took his arm. "C'mon," she said, "we'll take my car."

They arrived at the Albany Medical emergency entrance fifteen minutes later, literally running inside

56

when Eleanor saw two of Anne's police buddies standing at the admissions desk. One an angular-looking Hispanic, the other as Irish as Paddy's pig.

The room was filled with people either pacing or huddled into the plastic seats provided. She pushed past them, ran over and grabbed angular cop's arm. "How is she?" she shouted, her voice bordering on hysterics. "Is she all right?"

"She's okay, she's okay," angular cop quickly replied, looking her in the eye and placing a comforting hand on her shoulder. "She took two in the chest at close range so..."

Eleanor's eyes became ping-pong balls, her hands ran to her face and her voice rose two octaves. "She was shot twice in the chest? My God!" She stumbled backward.

"Whoa, whoa, whoa!" the Irish officer said, taking her elbow to keep her upright. "You didn't let him finish. Her bullet-proof vest held. Neither bullet went through. She's upstairs having an MRI to see if the blunt force impact caused any internal damage."

Not understanding, Eleanor stared blankly, "But you said the bullets didn't go through."

Angular cop nodded. "They didn't, but the impact can break a rib, damage the liver, or tear a hole in an intestine. Usually, it only leaves a bad bruise, but they always run tests to make sure."

An hour later one of the technicians entered the emergency room, sought them out and said, "Anne has been admitted and is resting comfortably. The close range of the bullets did some done damage—two cracked ribs— but there is no sign of internal bleeding." He raised the chart and with another look said, "In these cases she'll

57

likely be placed on medical leave for a while, but her doctor says she's expected to make a full recovery."

"Can we see her now?" Eleanor's father asked.

The tech nodded. "Yes, she's in room 305. I'll show you to the elevators."

When they entered her room, they were struck by the heavy odor of disinfectant and cloying smell of medicine. When Anne saw her father enter the room, she was startled. As startled as Scrooge coming upon Marley's ghost.

"Dad? What are you doing here?" she asked, slowly pulling herself up.

"What do you mean, 'What am I doing here?'" he snapped as he rushed to her bed and shrugged off his jacket. "I heard my daughter got shot. Where else would I be?"

Realizing he was being a little too harsh, he immediately apologized. "Don't mind me," he said. "Just a typical parental reaction. We're relieved to see our kid's all right while fighting the urge to dropkick their ass for scaring the hell out of us."

He placed his hand on the bar on the side of her hospital bed. She placed her hand upon his and looked up at him with those same sparkling green eyes she had from childhood. "Well, don't worry. I'm going to be fine," she said with a weary smile. "The doc says the ribs will heal quickly, and I'll be back on the job in about six weeks."

"Well, Dad's right," Eleanor said, coming around to the other side of the bed. "You gave us one hell of a scare, sis."

Anne groaned as she fully sat up, then smirked and said, "Well, I'll make your concerns my top priority the next time I'm dodging bullets." She reached over, grabbed the orange plastic pitcher, and poured a glass of water.

The two fellow officers entered and the question and answer period continued for the next ten minutes with Anne, as usual, dominating the conversation with assurances she was all right, that they shouldn't worry, and that everything was going to be fine. Once she saw that her assurances were finally sinking in, she gestured to the door.

"Now if you gentlemen will give me and my sister a moment, I need to discuss some things with her. You know, women things."

"I'll be right outside, honey," Anne's father said and kissed her cheek. The two officers waved and said they'd drop by again when their shift ended.

*

After the men left, Eleanor, with tear-filled eyes and streaked mascara, reached down and hugged her sister. "I was so scared," she whispered, holding her sibling tight, but not so tight as to hurt those cracked ribs. "So very scared. Especially since I've been short-tempered with you lately. I swear to God I will never leave the house again without telling you I love you."

After Anne hugged her and kissed her cheek, Eleanor stood and lovingly brushed some of Anne's blond hair from her face. "So what happened out there?"

Several moments passed before Anne answered. Eleanor watched as her sibling's face began a slow unsettling metamorphosis. Only moments earlier she seemed fine, a little beat up, but overall, fine.

She didn't look that way now.

She appeared to have aged ten years by the time she began her story. The ever-present sparkle behind her eyes went dark. It was as if the room temperature had dropped.

"When you start out as a cop," Anne began with a faraway look, her voice almost monotone, "they tell you to always trust your instincts. They drum it into you; drill it into your head. Use learn to use your instincts like ants use their antennae. Keeps you sharp, keeps you aware."

She took several deep breaths while splaying her fingers, nervously tapping the palms of her hands together. "The minute I heard the call, I knew I was going to be the first on the scene. Knew the situation would be critical; knew people would be dead."

Another deep breath.

"My instincts were right. When I arrived, the perps were in the front seats of the mini-van preparing to drive up the embankment when I swung in front, blocking their path.

"They tried ramming me out of their way, but my tires were wedged in the mud and for them, the pushing was all uphill. They soon gave up, but not without firing several rounds at me as the van rolled and slid on an angle down the muddy hill. Fortunately, even unmarked police cars are well-protected, so their bullets lodged into the passenger door panel and bullet-resistant glass.

As they regained control of the van and again attempted to climb up the hill, I jumped out, slid under my car, and fired at their front tires. Blew 'em both out. So now they're midway up the embankment and it's obvious—trying to climb it with two flat front tires won't work, so the guy in the passenger seat flings open the door and leaps out with his gun placed against this little girl's head. She couldn't have been more than six."

Stunned, Eleanor pressed her hands against her chest. "Good Lord, Anne, that's horrible!"

Anne bit her lip and continued. "It gets worse. I saw the kid's father lying at the bottom of the hill, partially covered in blood spattered leaves and pressed against the bushes, clearly dead. There was a crimson pool of blood surrounding what was left of his skull.

"I also notice, plastered on the back windshield of the mini-van were those white stick figures, you know, the stick figure dad and stick figure mom with their three stick figure kids, two girls and a boy and of course a stick figure dog, all smiling. Even the dog.

"I remembered thinking that a new stick figure had entered the picture—a stick figure man with the gun pressed against the older girl's head and he's not smiling. And the stick figure dad is dead, surrounded by white stick figure blood."

Eleanor's eyes filled with tears. "What did you do?"

Anne brought a tight hand to her mouth that slowly contracted into a fist. Her expression was taut, emotionless, detached. The fisted hand began to quiver, and seeing that, she dropped it to her side. "The guy called to me and said, 'Drop the gun and step away from the car or I'll shoot this kid! I mean it, I'll blow her fucking head off!'"

Another deep breath.

"Just then, the little sister sticks her head out of the mini-van's window and screams in panic, 'Please don't kill my sister!'"

"This diverts his attention for at best a second, but that second was an eternity to me,. In that little girl's face I saw your face, and in the face of the man at the bottom of the hill I saw Dad's. And in that split tenth of a second I

61

decided that by God and by all that is holy this evil fuck will not live to see another day, and so in that eternal second I took aim and fired, knowing I would not miss. And as that eternal second played out, his head vaporized into a fine red mist that momentarily hung over the kid's head like a scarlet halo. And as she leapt to the ground and the gunman fell backward dead, I drew a bead on the one behind the wheel. He's at a bad angle, so I move to the left to keep the family out of the line of fire, then shot through the windshield. I fired over and over and as I stormed toward him. Something struck my chest, knocking me back but I barely slowed because I wanted to see that red mist again. Needed to see that red mist again because in my mind's eye it's my father laying at the bottom of the hill and the words 'Please don't kill my sister!' are echoing in my head and I know this must end here and now. Then I saw the mother, sister and boy charge out of the now open-side panel door. I became momentarily concerned there might be a third gunman but instinctively, I knew there wasn't. The windshield was almost all gone as was most of the gunman's face but I keep firing and firing..."

Just then a middle-aged nurse entered, all business and stoic determination. She strode directly to Anne's bed and said, "The monitors alerted us to a spike in your pulse and blood pressure." She removed the cap from a syringe she brought in and emptied it into the clear liquid bag hanging to Anne's left. "That should take the edge off," she said with a smile as she recapped the needle. "You should start feeling the effects in a moment or two.

As the nurse left, Anne turned, looked out the nearby window and whispered, "Nice day. Glad I lived to see it."

She turned back, blinked slowly to focus then said, "What's going on with Dad? Just yesterday he was galloping around the back yard like the Monty Python crew on a quest and today, he seems like his old self. When I first saw him I thought I was hallucinating."

Eleanor grabbed a gray metal chair, pulled it alongside the bed and sat. "I had just come home from work when an officer showed up at the door and told me you'd been shot, and the first thing I did was run to Dad. I completely forgot that he's ill and would have no idea what to do."

Eleanor shook her head, dropped her hands into her lap and gave a bemused chuckle. "Geez Louise, can you believe that? I'm an executive vice-president who regularly signs off on million dollar transactions, have met with congressmen, senators, and judges, yet, when I hear my older sister is hurt, I go running to Daddy like a little girl. Kinda pathetic, don't you think?"

Anne started to sit up but found the meds had sapped her strength, so she grabbed the bed remote and pressed 'UP'. "I probably would have done the same thing," she said as the bed rose until the sisters were eye to eye. "So, what happened to make Dad normal again?"

Eleanor shoved her hands into her pockets, crossed her ankles and studied the floor. Her curly brown hair had fallen into her face. "When I told him you had been shot there was no reaction at first. He just stood there, staring. So I said it again. I said 'Anne's been shot!' And suddenly it was like watching someone coming toward you from far away. Somewhere deep inside, Dad's still there, and when it finally got through that you had been hurt, he fought his way to the surface. I could almost see the light of recognition in his eyes grow brighter and then, Boom!"

she said throwing her hands into the air, "that delusional soul became Dad again."

Anne's expression became dreamy. "Wouldn't it be nice if this little incident brought Dad back for good?" she asked. "I'd go through a hundred gun battles if it would bring him back to normal."

"Yeah, I would, too," Eleanor replied, then turned to the window and said, "Oh, by the way, Mom is going to stop by to see how you're doing." She said it so casually and matter-of-factly that the information didn't quite sink in at first.

Then it did!

"What the fuck!" Anne said, lurching forward and immediately grimacing from the pain."

As Anne gritted her teeth and pressed her hand to her side, Eleanor took the opportunity to calm the situation. She slowly stood, and with hands on hips and a no-nonsense expression, said, "Look, Annie (she always called her Annie when she was about to go head-to-head with her volatile sister), Mom saw the report on the news. Heard you got shot twice and called me in hysterics on my way here. C'mon, you had to know she would come to make sure you're all right. Geez, Dad straightened out and his head's made of Swiss cheese. So, nut up, put on your big girl panties and deal with it, okay? She probably only wants to see that you're all right and after some chit-chat, she'll be on her way."

With the sedatives calming the waters, Anne begrudgingly said, "Fine!" and lowered the mattress.

Then, looking over at her sister, Anne said, "I'm probably going to be released tomorrow, so I need you to bring me some stuff from home. My house keys are in my

64

purse over in that closet. Now listen carefully, I want you to get my…"

Chapter 10

He almost didn't notice it. It's very common to see an old newspaper lying on the benches of a bus stop or train station or any place you're stuck at with nothing to do but sit and wait. Normally, Jim August, Anne's and Eleanor's father, would have already returned home, now that he knew Anne was all right and the danger had passed. But they came in Eleanor's car, so he had to wait until she and Anne finished up.

He gave the newspaper a second look.

Ah, what the hell, he thought. *Maybe I'll do the crossword puzzle.* Confident he could bum a pen from the receptionist or one of the nurses, he scooched across the dull gray bench, snagged the edge of the paper with the tips of his fingers, and pulled it toward him.

He scouted for someone from whom I could borrow a pen, but everyone was either out of range or too busy.

He finally shrugged and decided to read the comics until someone came by.

Riffling through the ads and op-eds, he noted the many commentaries regarding 9/11, which struck him as odd because it had been well over a decade since that tragic day and if there were going to be commentaries about September 11, wouldn't they be more effective if they waited until 9/11 to print them?

Then he wondered why he had been outside without his wallet, keys or cell. He grew more concerned when he remembered that his car wasn't in the driveway.

He glanced at his feet.

And why am I wearing bedroom slippers without socks? he wondered. *And in the middle of the day for heaven's sake?!*

66

Something's wrong!

He grabbed the newspaper, flipped to the front page, read the date.

Thursday September 11, 20....

Feeling a cold chill, he flung the newspaper to the bench and slid away from it.

No, no. Calm down and put the pieces together. What's the last thing you remember doing before Eleanor told you Anne had been shot?

When he couldn't remember he grew panicky ... but then, the recollections started rolling in.

I was washing my car in the driveway. It was a beautiful day, a Saturday and... Anne was there... and...

He winced from a sudden, sharp pain in his head.

Focus, old man, focus! I was washing my car, yes. I'm sure of that. And Anne was there! But... but she was yelling at me!

Why was she yelling at me? And that look on her face! She was angry about something, but there was fear in her eyes too. Worry! That's what I saw. Fear and worry. And yelling. I definitely remember her yelling, but about what?

Wait! I remember now. She kept turning away and saying, 'What the hell are you doing? What's wrong with you? Put that away and get in the house. The neighbors will call the cops."

But that didn't make sense. *Why would the neighbors call the police on a guy hosing road grime off his car? I clearly remembered asking her that question.*

"Look what you're doing!" Anne kept shouting. "For heaven's sake look at what you're doing!"

He tapped his finger against his lips and recalled himself saying, *"I'm washing the dirt off my car. What's wrong with you?"*

67

Then she leaned in and said, "Look what you're doing it with!"

So I did and...

Oh, my dear God!

Just then an orderly passed and Jim asked him today's date and time.

The orderly smiled, pulled back his sleeve, looked at his watch and with a slight Latino accent said, "8:45 pm, September eleventh."

Jim's startled reaction to that information caused the orderly to become concerned. He reached down, took Jim's shoulder, studied his face and asked if he was all right.

He wasn't, not by any stretch of the imagination, but insisted he was fine. The reason for his distraught look however, was because he had suddenly recalled why Anne was yelling at him.

But what was even more frightening was that it had taken nearly ten seconds of scolding before he realized what he was doing. The embarrassment was so humiliating! But what was even more disconcerting was that event apparently occurred three months ago! *Where did those three months go? What had I done during that time? Good Lord, could I have brain cancer? Do the girls know about this?*

Adrenaline raced through his system. He felt his chest tighten, noticed it was getting hard to breathe... *Wait. Wait* he told himself, *remember what you told Eleanor, 'A crying person is a useless person. Solve the problem first, then cry all you want.' That's what I need to do before I lose it and start running down the hall screaming.*

He sat back and took a moment. *Maybe I had a reaction to some medication I'm taking. They warn you about that all the time on TV, 'Side effects may include this, that, and a couple of other horrible things' including the possibility it might actually kill you.*

His panic eased a little. A bad reaction to meds was a distinct possibility.

Then his brain reminded him of those three months he couldn't account for.

Hey, bartender, want to put a head on this sheer panic I'm feeling?

His mouth went dry, his stomach became a koi pond for piranha and he NEEDED to run. Run as far and as fast as humanly possible and not stop until this terror presently holding his heart in its cold, cruel hands fell far behind.

Then his brain threw another conundrum into the fire. *Do you know your name?* It asked.

Dear Lord, I'm drawing a blank, I don't even know my own... no wait, it's coming to me. My name is James Bennett August.

James Bennett August?

Wait! That doesn't sound right. That sounds made up. Or...or maybe it's just somebody who's name I know.

But then realized there was a way to check. He stood, turned, and looked at the patient list insert on his daughter's hospital door. It read Anne Ariel August. He felt a glimmer of hope when he also recalled that Anne, as a teen, used to refer to herself as "The Triple A of Babedom."

It all came rushing back. Like someone had inserted a backup program into his head and was downloading everything he had forgotten. Anne Ariel August, Eleanor Ivy August, ex-wife, Barbara Ellen August, nee Allen.

69

Good work, Jimmy boy, he told himself. *Good job holding on to your shit until you could piece things together. Must remember to tell Eleanor the meds are causing side effects and I have to stop taking them.*

Yes, his brain chimed in, *by all means tell Eleanor you're having a bad reaction to the meds. And to make an appointment with your doctor. You know, Doctor… And… uh, what's his name again? Oh and… oh yeah, there is that little mater of Anne's scolding. You weren't taking any meds then. In fact, you were on a health kick. You started eating right and exercising. You even stopped drinking. So what was really behind that little exhibition in the driveway? What's made you think you were washing your car when, in actuality, you had whipped out your pecker and was giving your Ford Mustang a golden shower? A momentary fugue state perhaps? A mini-stroke? Could it be…*

SATAN!?

He dropped his head into his hands. *Wait! There **was** a picture of a red devil with horns and a pointed tail, and witches and black cats …and a ghost picture. Oh, shit, that didn't happen three months ago—that was last Halloween. No, the last thing was… I think I was washing windows. Yes, I remember the blue bucket and the big yellow sponge. I was doing the annual spring cleaning and saw that Mrs. Harding's apple tree had these tiny green appl…*

"Dad…? Dad?"

He hadn't realized he had his face buried in his hands. When he looked up, he saw Eleanor standing over him, her jacket draped over her arm, her purse hanging from its thin strap, and her curly bonnet of brown hair highlighted by the fluorescent bulbs above.

She eyed him with concern. "Dad? Are you all right?"

70

When he didn't answer right away, she dropped to her haunches and studied his face. "Dad, do you know who I am?"

"Of course I know who you are." he said, wondering why she was asking.

"Then what's my name?" She was staring closely now, studying every line on his face, every movement, like a mother interrogating her kid when she suspects he's been up to no good.

"Eleanor... Ivy... August," he replied with sharp, clipped pronunciation.

Still eyeing him closely with her big blue eyes, she said, "And what's your name?"

Now clearly irritated he replied, "James Bennett August. And what's with the third degree?"

She took his hand, stood, and gently pulled him to his feet. "Time to go," she said. "Gotta pick up a couple of things for Anne on the way home."

He nodded and followed as she headed toward the elevators. She had just pushed the wall button and was putting on her coat when he asked her if he was on any specific medication.

"Some," she said as she again gave him the once over. Jim expected more details, but she didn't offer any.

The elevator arrived. They stepped in, the door slid closed, and as they began their descent, he said, "Well, what meds am I taking?"

She leaned against the wall. "Why do you ask? Don't you know?"

Her query to him was like a slap in the face. Like being the monkey in that 'Monkey in the Middle' game cruel kids play.

71

"Why don't you just answer the damned question?" he said sternly as the elevator slowed and the door opened. Two passengers entered, a smiling, middle-aged couple. The man was tall, gaunt, and wiry; the woman short, gray-haired and slathered in makeup. "Just got to see our first grandchild," the man said, beaming.

"That's wonderful," Eleanor replied, all chatty and smiling like they were old friends. "Boy or girl?"

"An eight-pound, two-ounce, baby girl," the woman announced proudly. "Our son said her name is Alicia May Hoppi…"

Jim had tuned them out because his brain had started in with the questions and accusations again. *Seems like Eleanor will do anything to avoid answering your question, old timer. Maybe she'll take these fine folks out for a congratulatory dinner! Maybe ask to see pictures of the baby? Anything other than tell you that you're old and in the way and that their mother was right to have run off with that beer guy, because it appears the ex dodged a bullet by unloading you before you became the burden to her that you are to your daughters.*

"Will you shut the fuck up?!" he said, not realizing at first that he had said it aloud, but did when Eleanor spun toward him in mid-sentence. She then turned back to the couple and while trying to come up with some explanation for his sudden outburst, the elevator, fortunately, came to rest at the lobby and the door opened.

"Well, congratulations again," Eleanor said, as she wrapped her hand around her father's arm and led him off the elevator. The still stunned couple managed a polite wave and took off in the other direction.

72

Once they were alone, Eleanor turned, "Why did you do that!?" she demanded as their footfalls echoed inside the cavernous hospital halls.

The loudspeaker clicked on: *Dr. McEnery code blue at 410! Dr. McEnery code blue at 410!*

"I'm sorry," he sputtered with embarrassment. "I was lost in thought, worried about Anne, and the dangers she faces every day and when I couldn't stop thinking about it, I snapped. That's about the best I can figure." He held up his hands and shook his head in exasperation.

She squeezed her eyes shut and sighed. "Well, all right then. I guess I understand. It's been a rough day."

As they stepped out of the hospital's front doors into the cool evening and made their way across the parking lot, he slowed the pace and said, "I got a couple of questions I need answered, and I need them answered before you drop me off."

She said nothing at first, nary a yes, no or 'go soak your head'. Finally, after fumbling around her handbag for her keys, she said, "Okay. When we get to your house, I'll answer your questions as best I can."

He nodded, smiled, and said "Thank you," but frankly, he didn't believe her. He didn't believe her at all.

Chapter 11

When they entered the house, Eleanor said she needed to use the bathroom. So, as she shrugged off her coat, dropped it on the hook behind the door and charged off to do her business, Jim slipped off his jacket and entered the living room. Once there, he casually draped his jacket on the arm of the couch and suddenly found himself directly eye-to-eye with his late son, Bob.

His breath caught in his throat.

It was only Bob's photograph, but it was the day's frightening events that made his eyes well up. He told himself he was doing what he had always taught his kids to do. Solve the problem first, then deal with emotions afterwards. But his emotions seemed out of whack. He was usually stable and consistent, but over the last few hours he felt as if his emotion were out of his control and careening from anger to melancholy to suspicion.

And so much had happened so fast. So many things didn't make sense.

He ran the heel of his hand against his eye. *Damn it, what the hell is wrong with me? Keep it together, Jim. Whatever is going on, you need to keep a clear head.*

He tried to divert his attention, tried to concentrate on something else. He was still determined to find out what medications he was on and what medical condition they were treating. He chose to focus on that.

But it didn't work. So many unpleasant memories. Hospitals, near death experiences, medications, another child's life in danger…

And in Bob's face he suddenly saw how much his son resembled Jim's own father.

Jim's old man wasted away in a VA hospital room, day after day, his body shrinking, aging, deteriorating, rotting. Visiting him inside those sterile walls for months as he'd rally and relapse, relay and relapse.

Jim was relatively young at the time, mid-twenties, and working as a musicians in Manhattan with his wife. Life was good, he was healthy and was beginning to draw attention as a songwriter. Still, every evening before heading to Manhattan he'd stop to visit his father.

Because he was a good son.

But as the seemingly endless visits to the hospital slogged on day after day...

...he began to wish it would just end.

It wasn't because he didn't love his father or had come to hate those daily treks. It was because his father was simply following the natural course of things. He lived a full life. Had done and seen everything he claimed he wanted to and so it wasn't as if anyone was being cheated.

But Bob was a very different story.

He was not far past twenty-one-years old when he, Anne and Eleanor noticed how easily Bob became fatigued. They thought it would pass but instead it grew worse, which deeply concerned them because Bob didn't get tired. Not now, not ever. The kid was a living dynamo of positive energy. Never had a bad or sullen attitude, not even during his teen years. Always positive, always forward looking, always determined to make the best of each and every day.

And there Bob was, right before his eyes, frozen in time. Staring out with that big friendly smile, the one that greeted Jim every morning. He could almost hear his son saying," Hey, Pop, how'd ya sleep? Want some coffee?"

Bob wasn't smiling the last time he saw him.

75

Jim paled and pressed his hand to his mouth, *Dear God, he was in agony. He had blankets piled on him and he still shivered, not from the cold but from the pain. There was nothing the doctors could do. I tried to take his mind off it; tried to get him to think of something else. Didn't work. Finally, he said, "I appreciate the effort. Dad. But you're not helping."*

Jim bowed his head. *Dad, you're not helping.*

Those words hurt him in ways that far exceeded anything physical ever could.

"He was my best friend, damn it!" Jim said in a rage as his hands balled into fists. "My only son," he whispered as tears ran down his face.

It didn't make any sense.

Bob's Smartphone app company had been successful. They had all invested and made money—good money. So good the house was paid off, the student loans cleared, credit cards made current and new cars paid for.

Anne was the first to move out. Fiercely independent and single-minded, she left as soon as she received her associate degree in criminology to join the Albany Police Department and rented an apartment nearby.

Eleanor followed soon after. Wildly ambitious, class valedictorian and armed with bachelor's degree's in both business and hotel management, she was heavily pursued by several hotel chains and accepted the offer from the Goldenrod Corporation. Although they were far from being one of the top hospitality firms, she saw an opportunity to get in on the ground floor of a concern that, if properly run, could make her lofty ambitions a reality.

Bob, although easily the richest, came home every weekend from college and finally, in his sophomore year, decided he had had enough. He had a boatload of money, yet didn't buy that expensive crotch rocket that was almost a prerequisite for yuppies his age, or get a cool bachelor pad. Instead, he said he liked living at home. He said most guys his age lived with roommates and since he and his father got along so well, he couldn't see the sense in spending time and money looking for something he already possessed.

Yeah, that's what he said, and yeah, Jim knew it was bullshit.

He was doing it for me, Jim recalled. *I knew that. Doing it because I had become solitary, sullen, and withdrawn.*

Following his wife's betrayal, Jim became suspicious of women. He bolted out of a relationship the moment he suspected something wasn't on the up and up. Hadn't made any new friends; didn't see any new people. He had gotten into the habit of coming home from work, eating dinner, then pounding beers till he fell asleep.

And why the hell not?! Jim thought. *I did my job. Got my kids through their teenage drama, into good colleges, and on to successful careers.*

Check, please.

But then Bob was done with college and that was that. Claimed it took too much time from his burgeoning app business. Jim tried to get him to reconsider. Tried to convice him that a college education was valuable regardless of the amount of money you possessed. Bob however turned a deaf ear. He made it clear he wasn't interested and that the topic was closed.

Once the two settled into a regular routine, Bob convinced Jim to join a divorced men's support group and resume jamming with other musicians. Got him playing tennis and golf and turned him on to video games. (Geez,

77

those things were addictive), and just as Jim started getting his life *back*…

…Bob began losing his.

Jim accompanied him to the doctor's offices, the hospitals, the imaging centers. Was right there every minute. Even as the disease ravaged Bob's body, even following the bone marrow transplant, Bob somehow maintained that strong, positive attitude.

As did Jim. But only for as long as Bob could see or hear him.

Once out of range Jim sobbed like a child with a scraped knee. But Bob never knew. Jim made damn sure Bob never knew. He'd put a bullet in his head before he'd allow his son to spend a single second worrying about how his illness affected his father.

Besides who gives a shit how I was handling it?! Jim recalled thinking. *Bob was the one who was dying.*

My best friend, my only son.

For months they went to the top specialists but the prognosis never changed. Hospital after hospital, from the jungle heat of summer, through to the sloppy, slushy winter.

Bob's cancer was particularly aggressive, vicious, and the percentage of survivors five years after diagnosis was barely in the teens.

My best friend, my only son.

As they were running out of options, Jim found himself growing annoyed at Bob's ever-present positive attitude. Jim was starting to think Bob viewed his own demise as inconsequential. Like Jim and Anne and Eleanor were just casual buddies he had spent some time with and was now looking forward to new places and new people.

78

Jim recalled they were walking through the parking lot toward Jim's car. It was a cold November evening and the sun had gone down. A light dusting of snow was falling and Jim's mood was grim. A particularly painful medical procedure they hoped might turn things around had been ineffective. Jim was rapidly becoming furious that such unspeakable horrors could befall someone as kind and personable and generous as his son. As they neared their car, Bob suddenly shrugged and said, "Well, nobody lives forever, I guess." and... well, Jim flew into a rage.

"You just don't understand, do you?" Jim thundered as he grabbed Bob's arm under the parking lot's sodium lamps, but immediately let go when he saw the painful expression on his son's face. "Your dying may not mean much to you," Jim said, "but it's ripping us apart."

He hadn't wanted to say that, let alone what followed. Looking back, he believed the terminal prognosis had made him hysterical. "You will leave a vacuum we'll feel for the rest of our lives," he said as tears welled. "And on each special family moment, the fact that you're not there to enjoy it will only make us miss you more. You have no idea how much you mean to us. The very thought of you dying saddens me in ways you couldn't possibly understand until you have a kid of your own."

Jim remembered he literally had to force himself to stop talking. He was teetering too close to the edge, so close that he was terrified he'd crack.

My best friend, my only son.

When Jim finished his spiel, he had no idea how his son would react. He wouldn't have been surprised if under the cold lights of the medical center's parking lot, Bob hauled off and slugged him. Wouldn't have been surprised if he grabbed him by the front of his jacket and said, "How

79

dare you? I'm the one dying you stupid, old bastard. Where do you get off telling me how I should face my mortality?"

But he did neither of those things. Instead he draped his arm over his father's shoulder and said, "I know how rough my illness has been on everyone, and I know how frightening losing me must be to all of you, but look at this situation from my viewpoint. If I die, you lose only one person. Just one. How would you feel if you were about to lose *everyone* you love? Every person you ever loved or cared for? Yes, losing one person is terrible, but I'm losing everybody. If I die, and I find myself in some sort of heaven, it won't mean a damn thing if I can't share its joys with my family and loved ones."

And that was when Jim couldn't hold back the tears anymore.

Afraid of becoming emotionally overwhelmed, especially when he needed to find out from Eleanor what his medical situation was, Jim left the living room, entered the kitchen and started making coffee.

The metal measuring spoons rattled as he measured in the ground decaf and the cupboard door creaked while being opened for the coffee mugs. He supposed Eleanor thought he was doing it to let her know he was becoming impatient, because she soon called out from her bedroom, "Be there in a minute. Just checking my email."

"Take your time," Jim called back, not meaning it.

He turned on the coffeemaker, leaned against the counter with arms folded and within seconds heard the water bubbling through the system. It was then he noticed the floral placemats on the kitchen table and several other items he didn't remember purchasing— and that uneasy hollow feeling returned.

But before it could secure its grip, Eleanor strode into the kitchen, tapping something into her cell phone. She looked up. "Just sending a quick e-mail to the office."

A moment later she tapped the send button and said, "That should take care of it," then put the phone away.

She had removed her pantsuit jacket top and replaced it with one of Jim's old sweaters. She looked so cute, her petite frame bundled into that bulky, oversized (at least for her) blue and white cable-knit sweater. She pulled out the blue vinyl chair from the kitchen table, sat and said, "All right. Let's get this done. What do you want to know about your medication?"

She had that all-business look she wore whenever she prepared to go into battle. Jim had seen it many, many times, particularly when she was a teenager and they'd go head-to-head over one issue or another. One time, she became so infuriated that her father was so much taller, she said, "Wait just one damn minute," stormed out of the room, grabbed a kitchen chair, returned, dropped it in front of him, climbed on it, and with them now at equal height, resumed the argument.

It was no surprise she rose through the business ranks quickly. She was tenacious as hell, and fought against all odds until she won. As this behavior became more evident, Jim, Anne, and Bob began referring to her as 'The Asp'.

Small but deadly.

Jim poured two cups of coffee and brought them to the table. Eleanor had drawn her knees to her chin and covered them with his bulky sweater. The tips of her little fingers peeked out from the ends of the sleeves.

81

They both drank it black with sugar and once the white crystals were ladled in, they each took a sip. "Okay, Dad, I'm going to give it to you straight," she said, then exhaled as if exhausted. "You came down with a viral infection that caused a swelling and deterioration in some areas of your brain. I'm not going to get into technical and clinical information; you can ask Dr. Gerritson tomorrow, I've called for an appointment, and they'll call me back in the morning with the time.

"Anyway, this condition causes you to slip into a fantasy world for, on occasion, extended periods. It has torn significant holes in your memory. The longer the spell, the less you remember. Anne and I have hired a caregiver to tend to you while we're at work. Her name is Mrs. Tuttle. She came highly recommended. Now as for the virus, it has no known cure. Which means…"

"Which means I'm not going to get better," Jim said, finishing her sentence as that hollow feeling began setting up camp and unloading supplies. "How many doctors have I seen, and what meds am I on?"

She gave a sad smile and pressed her steepled fingers to her mouth. "We've taken you to just about every specialist in the country, with no luck. You recently underwent an MRI and an acupuncture session in the hope it might clear your thoughts."

"Judging by your expression, it didn't help."

With welling tears Eleanor slowly shook her head.

"Am I dangerous?" Jim asked, closely watching her reaction. It was the hesitancy in her reply that sent the first pang of actual fear through him. He lurched forward. "I haven't hurt anyone, have I?"

Eleanor took a sip of her coffee and shook her head. "Not yet, but Mrs. Tuttle said that you swung at the MRI tech after the scan was complete which had us all concerned. Fortunately you missed, and we're all hoping it was a one-time thing."

As Jim took a steadying breath, he saw a tear slowly make its way down his daughter's cheek. The tips of her fingers trembled. He pressed his lips together, suddenly realizing how difficult this must be for her, and felt terrible for putting his littlest baby girl through this.

"How long do these spells last?" he finally asked. He wore a brave face, but the hard news about his illness was sinking in. He took a gulp of coffee, trying to drown the growing panic.

"This recent one lasted nearly three months. That is the longest episode so far." She reached over and squeezed his hand. "But it's so good to have you back. So good to be able to talk with you again."

He forced a smile and placed his hand over hers. "Are these spells getting progressively longer or does the amount of time I'm on..." He tried to come up with the right words, but settled on "... *Fantasy Island* vary with each occurrence?"

She squeezed his hand then let go, took a sip, stared off absentmindedly, then pulled out and lit a cigarette.

Jim wasn't sure if she was mulling over his question or refusing to answer. He listened to the low hum of the florescent lamp above and again sipped his coffee. Jim was never known for his patience and was nearing the point where he'd usually demand an immediate answer.

However...

Now that he knew he was suffering from some sort of brain disorder, Jim wasn't sure how to react. He didn't like the idea of guys with straitjackets dragging him away. He realized few things in life are as frightening as being

83

unsure of your sanity; of not being able to trust the thoughts coming into your head.

Turns out it was good that he waited.

"It varies," she finally replied, leaning in and flicking the ash into the ashtray. "I had to run them through my head because Anne is the one who keeps the records. But the length of time you're out of it definitely varies. The first one lasted seven weeks, then you were fine for nearly four months, then you were gone again for two weeks. In each case you were unable to remember what you did or where you were during what we refer to as your 'excursions,'" she said, making air quotes with her tiny fingers. "Can't you remember anything that happened over the past three months?"

Jim stared at the floor and said nothing, knowing his voice would betray his growing panic. It was so frighteningly unreal.

Three months couldn't have passed. How could I not know where I was or what I was doing for three entire months?!

His ability to cling to the remote possibility that all this was some elaborate gag was rapidly falling apart despite how much he needed it to continue.

You were pissing on the side of your car, his brain reminded him. *Was that an elaborate joke, too?*

"Dad?" Eleanor said, leaning in. "Does the name Turtledove mean anything to you?"

Jim put down his coffee cup. For reasons he couldn't quite comprehend, he immediately envisioned Anne, but somehow knew that wasn't right.

But it had to be.

But it couldn't be.

84

That hollow feeling was driving in tent stakes when he noticed his recollections weren't lining up like good little soldiers. No, they weren't good little soldiers at all!

"How about Bosco O'Bama the Third?" Eleanor asked as she pulled back the sleeves of the oversized sweater. Jim noticed her studying him, hoping, he supposed, for some kind of insight.

"There was a light…" he started, not aware at first that he was speaking. "A light on the window that reached into the sky. I remember staring at it for a long time, and it… it troubled me."

Eleanor again leaned in. "Dad, I don't follow. Did it have anything to do with Bosco O'Bama the Third?"

"Who's that?" he asked, not sure he had heard right.

Elle leaned back, clearly tired of pursuing the issue. "Doesn't matter. I told you what you wanted to know and tomorrow we'll stop by your doctor's office. He can fill you in regarding the meds and therapies." She drained the last of her coffee, then rose from her chair

"Okay," Jim said, picking up his cup to take it to the sink. "You go home and get some sleep. Give me a call in the morning and let me know what time the doctor's appointment is."

Eleanor smiled, walked over (her white slippers slapping the linoleum floor), placed her hand on her father's shoulder and gave it a friendly pat. "I'm going to spend the night here, in my old room," she said, lovingly gazing into his eyes. "I have some last-minute work to do for an appointment in the morning, after which I'll drive you to Dr. Gerritson."

That name still didn't ring a bell, but Jim didn't let on. Instead, he smiled and pressed his hand on top of hers. The

85

thought of having at least one of his kids under his roof for the night took some of the sting out of the day's madness.

She got up on her toes, kissed his cheek and said, "Good night, Dad. See you in the morning."

He returned the kiss, and she headed out of the room.

As Jim turned off the kitchen lights and went to draw the blinds, he saw his car wasn't in the driveway and called out to Eleanor as she climbed the stairs.

"Elle," he called out, "where's my car? It's not in the driveway."

"I'm tired, Dad, it's been a long day," she called back in a noticeable 'I-don't-feel-like-answering-any-further-questions,' voice. "We'll talk in the morning." With that Jim heard her door close.

Standing there, he wondered if he should let it go. He tried to convince himself to let it go but that simply was not his way. He had always been tenacious. Once he saw a chink in the armor, he didn't stop until it was all stripped away. His daughter Anne was the same way; probably was what made her such a good detective.

Jim started climbing the stairs. "Eleanor, just tell me where my car is. That thing cost $32,000 and that's a hell of an investment. Did I wreck it? Was it stolen?" he asked as he approached her door. "Was it…"

He heard the very audible click of Eleanor's door lock.

His eyes widened. His heart dropped.

In all the years she lived in that house, over all the fights and disagreements and damn near fisticuffs she and Jim had, she never once felt the need to lock her door.

Jim opened his mouth.

Nothing came out. He just stood there.

She's afraid of me. Afraid I might harm her while in one of my fugue states.

86

And it was at that moment that all the tenacity, all the determination, all the go-go-go drive to find out what happened to him and fix it, slipped away like the final breath of a dying man.

With a heavy heart, Jim slowly plodded down the stairs and into the living room. Didn't bother to turn on the lights as he entered—just kicked off his shoes, laid down on the couch and said a prayer. And in that prayer he asked God to take him out of the picture and to erase this horrific, miserable day from his memory. This day where his oldest daughter reacted to his arrival at her hospital bed with the surprise of watching a dead man do the chicken dance and where his youngest locked her bedroom door out of fear. This soul-killing day where he discovered all the effort he had made over the years to be a good father, a good husband and a respected member of his community, had all been for nothing.

Nothing!

"They never forget the end of a movie!" Jim recalled hearing some famous director say. "They may love it, hate it or be indifferent but it's the ending that stays with them. It's the final moments they remember."

As he placed the throw pillow under his head, he thought of his own father.

It's funny, he thought. *When I do think of him, I don't automatically recall the time he took me go-cart racing on my twelfth birthday, which was one of the happiest days of my life, or the time he saved a woman who was struck by a car and left for dead. I showed all my friends at school the newspaper story about him. Had his picture with the word Hero as its headline. Or the time he tackled a thief who punched an old lady and ran off with her purse. Or that*

87

fact the he had always been a good husband, father and provider.

Yeah, there were a lot of great things about my father, but the first thing that always comes to mind is him telling me in a rage not to bother coming back to the hospital.

He died hating me.

And I hated him for that. Couldn't help it.

They never forget the end of the movie.

I suppose my daughters will feel the same when I go.

Or maybe just relief.

And so Jim asked again, "Dear God, please put an end to this."

Chapter 12

The moment Elle's alarm clock sounded, she spun around and slapped the off button. She had been drifting in and out of sleep all night trying to figure out a way to explain to her father what *did* happen to his car, as well as the fate of a lot of other things he once owned. But it was far too early for her to deal with that now. Hopefully she would have a fully formed explanation by the time she picked him up for his doctor's appointment.

She rose from bed, quickly dressed, put on a minimum of makeup and hoped to make it down the stairs and out of the house before her father woke and started asking more questions.

As she stealthily eased her way down the stairs, the sight of her father fast asleep on the couch sent a momentary jolt of concern. She immediately tried to figure out how she could quietly gather her things and get out of the house without waking him.

No easy task. Every since Bob died, the slightest sound would pull him from even the deepest sleep.

Now, with coat, pocketbook and car keys in hand, along with her briefcase, she slowly unlocked the kitchen door and winced when the bolt snapped back with an audible click. She threw a quick glance to the living room and awaited that inevitable calling of her name. However, it didn't come. Apparently, she thought with a smile, this was going to be one of the those very few times she would be able to slip out of the house without her father's knowledge. A trick she had tried to master throughout her teens, with very little success.

Once outside, she climbed inside her car, put the keys in the ignition and stopped, realizing that starting the engine of her powerful Corvette would have her father up and at the door in a matter of seconds, she instead released the parking brake, put the car into neutral and let it slowly roll down the driveway and into the street with nary a sound.

Now far enough away to make a clean getaway, she started the engine and took off grinning from ear to ear.

"Sorry," Eleanor said as she charged through the door to Anne's hospital room, "I'm a little late. Dad peppered me with questions when we left here last night like he usually does when he rejoins the living, so I thought it best to take him straight home. I found him sleeping on the couch when I got up. Obviously he wanted to continue the questioning before I left for work. Fortunately I managed to tip-toe out before he woke up, then had to fight traffic on my way to your apartment."

Anne sighed and nodded. Her blank, far-away expression betrayed her lack of interest.

"Anyway," Eleanor said, holding up a brown paper bag as she shook off her coat, I got everything you wanted. So hang out, watch TV and chill until they release you. Any idea when that's going to be?" She pulled over a chair and draped her coat over the back.

Anne shook her head and ran her thumb and index finger over her lips.

Eleanor studied her sibling. "What's with you?" she asked. "For heaven's sake you're not feeling guilty about the guys you shot, are you?"

Tears welled in Anne's eyes. She quickly wiped them away and again shook her head.

Eleanor snarled. "Well, I certainly hope not. Rat bastards murdered those kids' father right before their eyes

90

and probably would have killed that little girl too, if it wasn't for you. Dirty scumbags deserved everyth…"

"It's not because of them," Anne said, turning toward her. "I was just told that an investigation is being made into the shooting and that I'm suspended until it's completed."

Eleanor was stunned. "What! An investigation for what? They were shooting at you. You were hit twice! What's there to investigate?"

Anne shook her head. "It isn't the department that is demanding an investigation, it's Mrs. Blanchet, the mother of the family I saved. She's claiming I put her and her family at risk by continuing to fire at the driver of the mini-van after it was clear he was dead. Said the bullets could have ricocheted and struck her or one of her children."

"That bitch!" Eleanor shouted, loud enough to grab the attention of the visitors passing their room. "That fucking bitch!" Red-faced she slammed his fists to her sides. "You risked your life to save her and her children and she wants *you* investigated?"

Anne wiped her eyes. "She's claiming my interference was reckless. She said the carjackers were preparing to let them go when I showed up."

Eleanor was gap-jawed. "But they killed her husband!"

Anne nodded. "Yes, but the woman is saying her husband's death was an accident. Says when the attackers ran them off the road, all they demanded was their van and money, but her husband caught one of the carjackers off guard with a punch and as he reached for carjacker's gun, the other one shot him."

91

With a look of astonishment Eleanor dropped into the chair. "Unbelievable. It's like the old saying—no good deed goes unpunished."

With her hand pressed to her forehead, Anne said, "So the mother is suing the department for six-million dollars. The department lawyer said that if it is proven that I acted inappropriately, she could win and I would be fired. Maybe even face negligence charges."

"Have you given a statement?" Eleanor asked automatically reaching for a cigarette. When she realized where she was, she yanked her hand out of her jacket in frustration.

Anne pulled herself up and swung her feet over the side of her bed. Her long, blond hair hung bedraggled over the shoulders of her white hospital gown, her face was pale and quite plain. It was as if the events of the past twenty-four hours had sucked away all of her natural beauty. "No, not yet," she said, pushing her hair behind her ears. "The lawyers say any statement I give while under pain medication would be inadmissible. So it probably won't happen until the end of the week."

Eleanor reached over and pressed her hand on her sister's arm. "Remember what Dad would say when we were teens and were heading out to a party or something?"

Anne thought for a moment. "You mean about never telling the police anything without having a lawyer present?"

Eleanor nodded vigorously and sat down on the bed beside her sister. "That's right, and damn good advice it is. I've worked with a number of sharp lawyers over the years, and I'm sure I'll have no problem lining up a heavyweight, not only to represent you, but to drag that money-grubbing bitch over the coals. Seriously, Anne," she said, raising her hand to her sister's shoulder. "Don't let this get to you. It's like Dad always says, 'Don't fall down until you're hit.'"

Anne chuckled a little. "You know, the two of us quote Dad like most people quote Confucius."

Eleanor shrugged. "Well considering how well we turned out, it appears the old man knew a thing or two. Did a damn good job raising us. Which reminds me, how did it go with Mom last night."

Anne tilted her head from side to side seemingly unable to come up with the proper response. "It was okay I guess," she finally replied, casting her eyes to the floor. "With the sedatives cruising through my system I didn't have the energy to get as angry as I usually do. So we talked like you said, just chit-chat, nothing important until she mentioned that it was in this very hospital where Grandpa August killed himself."

Eleanor leapt off the bed and turned to her sister, her sudden movement knocking her pocketbook to the floor, spilling her lipstick, car keys and other select items. "Wait! What? Why would she say Dad's father killed himself?"

Anne drew in a deep breath and slowly let it out. "Apparently, there was more to the story than we were told. Mom said it was true that Grandpa August did ban Dad from the hospital and yes, he really didn't know that it was dad and not Uncle Dan who came every day. But apparently he DID know what a burden he was putting on the family physically, emotionally, and financially. Two days after Grandpa banned Dad, the old guy slipped into the janitor's closet in the middle of the night, and using a flat sheet, hanged himself from the overhead water pipe. The janitor found the body early the next day."

93

Eleanor rolled her eyes and shook her head as she bent over and gathered the things that spilled from her pocketbook. "You know, this family goes through the craziest shit. Sometimes I think we're direct descendants of the Addams family". She stood and said, "So how did it play out?"

"Mom says neither Grandma nor Dad wanted to make an issue out of it. In return for not suing the hospital for negligence, the cause of death was listed as advanced necrotic liver disease and his remains were quickly cremated."

Eleanor slapped her hands against her thighs and said, "Unbelievable!" and was about sit back down on the bed when a thought struck her. "Oh, before I forget, I wanted to ask you, now that Dad's normal again, what do you want to do with Mrs. Tuttle?"

Anne eyebrows raised. "Hadn't thought of that," she replied. A moment later she added, "Best not do anything. If we let Tuttle go, she'll easily get another job and if he relapses…"

"*When* he relapses, Anne," Eleanor reminded her.

Anne gave a quick nod. "Yeah, you're right. So let's hold on to Tuttle."

"Okey-doke," Eleanor replied, eager to get outside and light up a smoke. She reached to the back of the chair for her coat. "I'll have a lawyer lined up for you within a day or so. In the meantime don't tell anybody anything. Not your friends, and certainly not your cop buddies."

"What if *you're* called to the stand and asked to repeat this conversation?" Anne asked, suddenly concerned.

"Didn't I tell you?" Eleanor said sliding into her jacket. "I'm going to be in Kuala Lumpur that week."

Anne eyed her sister suspiciously as Eleanor gave her a wink and made her way out.

Chapter 13

Mrs. Tuttle was stunned to find the front door locked, and even more surprised when, after knocking, the door opened and before her stood Jim 'Gam'pa' August. He was wearing his light blue pajamas and slippers and his expression of surprise made it clear he had no idea who she was.

Seeing a bright red line—that she later learned was ketchup—running from his left shoulder to the chest muscle area of his PJs, she quickly pushed past him and nervously looked around the living room and into the kitchen. Not seeing anyone, she spun toward Jim, "Where are Anne and Eleanor?" she demanded.

He eyed her in amazement. "Excuse me, but I don't remember inviting you in. And I certainly don't appreciate..."

"Shut up!" she said, storming toward him. "Now I'm going to ask you just one more time, where are Anne and Eleanor?!" Her face was grim and reddening, her voice a deep growl.

Not one to back down from confrontation, Jim folded his arms and said, "None of your damn business, lady. Now get out of my house!"

Ignoring him, she turned and charged into the kitchen. On the wall was a landline the daughters kept connected even though they both had cell phones. It was one of the few things their father still remembered how to use while on his excursions.

Growing increasingly annoyed, Jim quickly followed.

"Last chance," she said as she grabbed the receiver from the beige wall phone. "Tell me what you've done with Anne and Eleanor or I'm calling 911 right now."

Stunned, Jim held up his hands and said, "What I've done? What are you crazy?" he asked, seriously considering the possibility that she might well be, or the other possibility that he was having one of his hallucinations. "The girls are fine, although I still have no idea why that should be any concern of yours."

"Where…are…they?!" Tuttle demanded. Hard-faced, she held the phone receiver like a barbell in a closed fist.

"All right, I've had enough of this!" Jim said and stepped toward Mrs. Tuttle. She immediately grabbed the heavy iron skillet from the stove with her free hand, raised it above her head and made it clear she'd open his skull if he came a step closer.

Drawing back, Jim thundered, "Who the hell are you, you crazy bitch!?"

"My name is Mrs. Tuttle. Anne and Eleanor hired me as your caregiver."

Jim immediately dropped his hands, rolled his eyes, exhaled and lowered his head. "Ooohhh," he said with one of those *so-now-she-tells-me* look. "The girls *did* mention you. Had they told me to expect you today, we could have avoided all this drama."

She kept the skillet raised above her head. "I don't trust you," she said, coldly eying him. "Go into the living room, I'm going to call Eleanor."

Jim was going to say that wouldn't be necessary but having learned he almost punched out a MRI tech, he felt her fear was justified.

Apparently this women is one tough cookie.

Figuring it best if they returned to their neutral corners, he simply nodded and left the room.

Minutes later, Mrs. Tuttle exited the kitchen. "Sorry about the mix-up," she said, tying her apron over the front of her slacks. "But caregivers who tend to dementia patients are taught never let our guards down or believe anything the patient says without verification. I wasn't aware you had... gotten your facilitiess back, or of Anne's close call with those carjackers. I'm so relieved she's all right." she said as she began wandering around the room tidying. She opened a paperbag she had brought in from the kitchen and emptied the ashtray into it.

"Eleanor said to tell you she scheduled a doctor's appointment this afternoon with Dr. Gerritson. Says she'll pick you up at 1:30."

"Okay," Jim said, dropping candy wrappers from the end table into the bag. "Look, would you mind taking a seat. I'd like to ask you a couple of questions."

She eyed him, but gave no indication she was willing to comply.

"Please," he said, gesturing to the couch.

After a moment, she gave a quick nod, sat, placed the cup and dish in her lap and laid the paper bag on top of them.

Jim clasped his hands and took on a thoughtful pose. "You were pretty aggressive in the kitchen, Was that really necessary? Wouldn't it have been easier to try and reason with me?"

She immediately scowled, leaned in and said, "No. Any other questions?"

Startled by her bruskness, Jim wondered if this woman had abused him while he was in his fugue state. He doubted she would admit it if she had, but decided to ask anyway. "Have you ever struck me, while I was in your care?"

98

She nodded and with a smile replied, "Sure, plenty of times."

Clearly taken aback, he then asked, "So you think it's okay to abuse an emotionally troubled person?" he asked.

She shrugged and sighed, "Do you think you're qualified to critique my actions when I have over twenty-five years of experience with people like you? And that my actions have managed to keep you from being tossed in the looney-bin even though you have, on several occasions, proved you are a danger not only to yourself but to everyone around you?"

With a stern expression Jim said, "Well, regardless of your experience I'm going to tell my daughters that I don't want you as my caregiver. You're clearly insensitive and abusive."

Mrs. Tuttle shrugged and said, "Yeah, well go shit in your hat." And with that she got up, and headed determinedly across the room and toward the kitchen.

Stunned, Jim said, "Okay, well that tears it, you're fired. I want you out of this house immediately!"

Charging through the swinging door to the kitchen and giving no indication that she heard a word he said, she dropped the bag into the garbage, placed the cup and dish in the sink, then called out, "What do you want for breakfast?" She opened the refrigerator door. "You got a choice between an egg and spinach omelet, apple cinnamon oatmeal or orange juice and a bran muffin."

"Hey!" Jim shouted, storming into the kitchen. "I said you're fired and I want you out of my house!" He pointed at the kitchen door.

She spun around and placed her hands on her hips. "Yeah, and I said, 'Go shit in your hat.' Try to remember, mush brain that I work for Anne and Eleanor. Only they

99

can fire me and that's something they won't be doing that anytime soon."

"Fine," Jim snapped. "Well then, I'll call the police and have you physically removed from the premises."

"Okay, you do that, but in the meantime, what'll it be for breakfast?" she replied, leaning against the kitchen counter.

Furious at her casual indifference, he stormed over to the wall phone and grabbed the receiver.

She sighed, and, shaking her head in exasperation, plodded over and dropped down into a seat at the kitchen table. "I wouldn't make that call if I were you."

"Yeah, well, you're not me," he said, placing the receiver to his ear and wondering if he should dial 911 or the operator for the number of the local precinct.

"Fair enough," she countered with that noticeable inflection people use when they know how something is going to end. "But if you make that call you will never be permitted to enter this house again."

He let the hand holding the phone drop to his side. "And what's that supposed to mean?"

"Just this," she said, standing and approaching. "Although you don't know it, this won't be the first time you've called the police on me. And we've had this exact conversation about my treatment of you, not just once, but twice before. The last time the police arrived, they told your daughters that perhaps it was time they put you in a full care facility. If you call them again, they'll insist upon it.

"Now you may not believe me, but each time your virus flairs up, it physically damages you. Back when you were first diagnosed you were able to remember people and events you experienced after you became ill. That's no

100

longer the case. I've been your caregiver for just about a year and each time you revert to normal you have a new gap in your memory. The longer the excursion, the larger the gap. Since you don't remember me, I'm betting you don't know what you were doing just before you went off on your last trip to happy land, do you?"

Jim was going to tell her he was washing his car but that wasn't really true—and the true story was just too embarrassing.

"Time's up!" she said. "You were helping me wash the windows when all of a sudden you started talking about some guy with balloons, something about an amusement park and for some reason, you thought I was Anne."

Jim's eyes widened.

Mrs. Tuttle wiped her hands on her apron and folded her arms, placed her thumb and index finger to her chin and said, "Still want to make that call?"

Receiving no answer, she walked back to the refrigerator, "So," she said with a backward glance, "what have you decided on for breakfast?"

Jim was almost sure she was bluffing. Almost sure she made the whole thing up.

But he couldn't take the chance.

He hung up the phone.

At promptly 1:30 pm Eleanor arrived at the house. Mrs. Tuttle was in the kitchen gathering the lunch dishes.

"Hello, Mrs Tuttle. Is my father ready?"

The caregiver hooked her thumb toward the bedroom. "Yeah. He's in his room, pissed off that he can't fire me."

Eleanor exhaled exhaustedly and shook her head as she dropped her pocket book and car keys on the table. "I'm so sorry, Mrs. Tuttle," she said as she shook off her

101

jacket and hung it on the door hook. "And I apologize again for not warning you what to expect. Since he sees you every day, I forgot that he might not know who you are. I've been playing catch-up ever since yesterday's excitement and clearly dropped the ball. Again I'm sorry."

Mrs. Tuttle finished loading the rinsed dishes and utensils into the dishwasher and closed the door. As she turned the dishwasher on, she said, "It's really nobody's fault, We're all flying by the seat of our pants, but now that he's back, please explain to him that he's not qualified to question how I handle him. And that his hippie-dippie, 'be cool and chill, man', suggestions on how I should do my job are insulting and unwelcome."

Eleanor's bowed her head. "I will talk to him. And I will make him understand that he has to do what you tell him, or Anne and I will have him institutionalized."

With a quick nod, Mrs. Tuttle indicated that she was satisfied and resumed her kitchen duties.

*

As Eleanor drove her late-model cherry red Stingray Corvette toward Dr. Gerrittson's office, she broached the topic of Mrs. Tuttle with her father.

"You've got to get rid of her!" he said sternly, folding his arms.

Eleanor shook her head, "No can do, Dad. She's the best at what she does, and more importantly, she keeps you safe."

He turned to her, his face wide with surprise. He stared at her for a moment, then said, "Eleanor, she actually admitted that she physically struck me on several occasions! That's patient abuse and she should have her license revoked. People with brain illnesses should be

102

treated with compassion and understanding, not physical harm."

She eyed her father for a moment and replied. "I love you Dad, more than life itself, but you have no idea what you're talking about."

Jim jerked back. "What? So you're okay with her physically hurting me?"

Eleanor sighed, "When necessary, yes!" she said curtly. "Do you have any idea how many times you've tried to hurt Mrs. Tuttle? That you attempted to push her down the stairs? That you've thrown food at her, hot coffee at her, and tried to slam her hand in a car door?"

Although startled to hear this, Jim countered with, "Well perhaps if she wasn't hurting me, I wouldn't try to hurt her."

Eleanor shook her head. "But that's the point. Dad. You weren't trying to hurt *her*. In all those instances, you were in another place, dealing with a completely different reality. Each day you have extensive conversations with imaginary people. You ride imaginary horses, feed imaginary animals, flee from imaginary volcanoes, have shoot outs with imaginary mafia hitmen, Nazi's and Osama bin Laden even though he's been dead for years."

He shot her a condescending look. "What? That's ridiculous!"

"No!" she shot back. "That's the absolute truth. Mrs. Tuttle is irreplaceable because she anticipates these actions and knows how to defuse them. When you attempted to strike a female MRI tech with a closed fist, Mrs. Tuttle saw it coming and shoved you off balance . If she hadn't, you would either be in jail right now, or in a psych ward. And we'd be sued for everything we have, which would make it impossible to pay for your care."

103

She reached over and placed her hand on her father's shoulder. "It's far more complex than you realize, and having Mrs. Tuttle makes it easier for Anne and I to go to work without having to worry if you're going to attack the UPS man because you think he's a terrorist with a bomb."

Jim huffed and turned away. "Why can't we hire someone else for the job? Especially since I have such a strong dislike for her."

Eleanor gave a quick shake of her head and reached over to turn on the car's heater to offset the autumn afternoon chill. "Not going to happen, so let's just drop it. Talk to Dr. Gerritson about your condition," she said as she pressed the signal indicator for a right turn and slid into the exit lane. "Maybe if you knew more about it, you'd understand why Anne and I won't fire Mrs. Tuttle."

Jim was furious at Eleanor's dismissive attitude. He owned the house. He worked like a dog for years to keep up the mortgage payments until their family's investment in Bob's app company solved their financial problems. So why was he allowing his youngest daughter to call the shots? *Perhaps,* he thought, *I'll just sell the house and move to Florida. Tell that bitch Tuttle to go shit in her own hat. Really, why should I put up with this nonsense? When I get to Florida I could hire my own caregiver. One that isn't an abusive bitch.*

Jim's stern expression lessened as he stared out the window as they approached the medical center's parking lot. *Yeah, I just might do that after all!*

After the initial physical was completed and blood taken, Jim sat on the examination table amid the cold steel and sterile environment as Dr. Gerritson checked his blood pressure. "It's a little high," he commented as he eyed his

104

watch and timed Jim's pulse, "but I don't think you'll require medication yet. But likely soon." As he continued with the examination, Jim mentioned how uncomfortable he was with Mrs. Tuttle and that he was considering selling the house and moving to Florida.

Gerrittson's sudden panicky facial expression caught Jim off guard. The doctor quickly removed the blood pressure cuff and said, "I have videos of you while you were in your fugue state," he said with deep concern. "I hesitate to show them to you because, well, frankly, you're a bit fragile. But after hearing your plans, I think you should have a look. It might change your mind about Florida."

Videos?

Jim leapt at the chance. He wasn't entirely convinced his condition was as bad as everyone indicated. Perhaps these videos would prove it.

With a new attitude Jim hopped off the examination table and reached for his shirt and pants on the nearby chair. "By all means, doc, let's have a look."

As Jim dressed, Gerritson wrote notes on his clipboard and said, "I'll have my nurse set it up then take you to the video conference room. While you watch, I'll update your daughter on your condition."

Jim nodded as the doctor exited, then slowly slid his arm into the right sleeve of his shirt, careful not to catch it on the adhesive bandage covering the needle mark. After checking his hair in the mirror and slipping a 'How to control your high blood pressure' pamphlet into his pants pocket, he walked into the hall and followed the attending nurse to the video conference room.

105

"So what's the prognosis, Doctor?" Eleanor asked as Gerritson entered. She was sitting in his office in front of his desk and had just zipped her pocketbook to keep the physician from seeing the pack of cigarettes inside. "He seems to be doing better."

As Dr. Gerritson came around to his seat, his tight-lipped expression and furrowed brow made it clear he didn't agree. "According to the MRI, his condition is steadily deteriorating."

That removed the casual, breezy expression from Eleanor's face. "Oh... I see." she said, suddenly concerned. She rolled her hands and wished she could light up a smoke.

The physician leaned in and ran his palm over his thinning gray hair. "The medical test results fall right in line with the weekly reports your Mrs. Tuttle forwards. I'm not surprised he swung at the MRI tech. He likely became overwhelmed by the frustration of not being able to fully comprehend what's going on around him."

She placed her hands on the edge of the desk. "But," she protested, "over the last twenty-four hours he's been his old self. Strong, clear-headed, decisive. You and Mrs. Tuttle keep saying he's getting worse but from what I'm seeing, he's on his way to a complete recovery."

"Ms. August," Gerritson said, clasping his hands and wearing that look one has when about to deliver bad news, "we've had this conversation before. We both know that's simply not possible. At least not without some medical miracle. And yes, he appears completely lucid, but remember, these events can last for months, minutes and sometimes switch back and forth at random. My point is, he can't be left alone in an uncontrolled environment under any circumstances because there is no pattern for his

106

condition. You have to come to terms with this, Ms. August," he said this with a taut face and an 'I'm-not-looking-to-upset-you-BUT,' expression. "The virus has infected and swollen certain motor and involuntary areas of his brain. As the disease progresses it will bring on bouts of vomiting, sneezing, and hiccupping. As it reaches its final stages, there *will* come a point when it will no longer be able to send the necessary autonomic signals that keep the lungs working and the heart beating. When that happens, he will simply… "

"He asked me about his meds," Eleanor interrupted, knowing full well what he was about to say and not wanting to hear it. She was determined not to become emotional, even though the bleak diagnosis upset her. "He believes his condition may be a side effect of his medication."

Gerrittson's smirk showed his utter dismissal of that possibility. He placed his arms on the desk and shook his head. "No, I assure you it's not the meds, though there *is* a new medication available that, well I won't bore you with the technical details, but it is an anti-inflammatory. Recent recent clinical trials have shown it reduces the length of hallucinatory episodes. I'll write him a prescription."

At that moment the nurse passed the doorway. "Nurse," he called out.

She stepped back and poked her head in. "Yes, Doctor?"

"Has Mr. August finished the videos?"

She checked her watch. "Should be just wrapping up."

"Thank you," the doctor replied. As the nurse left, he said, "You go collect your father and I'll have the prescription waiting at the reception desk."

"Okay," Eleanor replied. "And thank you, doctor." She picked up her pocketbook, and went to retrieve her father.

Eleanor had hoped for better news but on some level knew some miracle—medical or otherwise—hadn't occurred, and it was only a matter of time before Dad donned his pith helmet and marched off for whatever land he lived in during his time 'away'.

When she reached the video room, she opened the door and was about to say, "Ready to go, Dad?" but stopped dead when she noticed her father staring intently at the large, blank TV flat screen. What was even more disconcerting, was that every few seconds, he'd burst out laughing.

She cleared her throat, and her father turned. He appeared normal enough so she said, "Ready to go?"

He smiled and said, "Just let me finish watching this cartoon, then we'll get our coats and go with you." He turned back to the television.

She felt a shiver.

The TV screen was black. The DVD player tray had opened revealing the shiny silver disk.

We'll get our coats and go with you?

She started toward her father. "Is there somebody with you?"

He shrugged and shook his head. "It's just me and Bosco O'Bama the Third."

She spun around and called out, "Doctor!"

*

Jim had been absolutely flabbergasted by what the video revealed. He ran his hand through his hair several times as he sat on the edge of the leather couch, then pressed his hands to the side of his face. It was as if a

108

seriously disturbed man had commandeered his body and was playing like a child in a Batman costume.

That is me! he thought as he extended his arms in disbelief. There was no escaping that fact. There he was, running around the back yard, talking to himself, pointing in various directions as if explaining to his invisible companion what had caught his interest.

In later parts he charged forward as if in battle, his hand fashioned like a gun. Firing wildly at imaginary assailants. In another part, he slapped rapidly at his clothes, then dropped and rolled as if on fire.

Jim was a mere thirty seconds into the video when he realized there would be no selling his house, no moving to Florida, no driving around the Adirondack Mountains in his canary yellow Ford Mustang with the top down and the radio blaring. No more family vacations, no more dining at fine restaurants, no more wine tasting at upstate vineyards. No more ski trips or sea cruises.

And there would be no firing of Mrs. Tuttle.

The actions of the man in the video were so bizarre, so unlike him, that Jim tried to convince himself that some look-alike actor had been hired to perform these ridiculous antics as some sort of gag reel.

But the longer the DVD ran, the more horrifying and unfunny those 'gags' became.

With his arm pulled tight against his chest and his hand pressed to his mouth, the more *real* it became.

But throughout, he always appeared to be in the company of a much smaller person. Jim believed it was a child because his video self often sat on his haunches when involved in conversation. Patted the air at his side as if showing affection. Held out his hand for that invisible child to take.

I am much, much sicker than I thought, and I owe Mrs. Tuttle an apology. And I must thank the girls for not having me put away and for having that tall backyard fence installed. If the neighbors ever got an eyeful of what I was doing, they'd insist I be committed.

Dear God, he prayed. *My daughters have done more than enough. Please take me out of the picture. Please put an end to...*

..."What 'cha doing, Pop-Pop?" Bosco O'Bama the Third asked. "I'm not interrupting one of your prayer rituals am I? Cause I can come back."

I turned to see my wonderful grandson with his flaming red hair and gap-toothed smile, tugging at a stick of beef jerky. He wore an Indiana Jones T-shirt, jeans and the cowboy boots on his feet swung back and forth as he sat beside me on the couch.

"No! No!" Of course not!" I said with a beaming smile. "I'm always glad to see you, you little scamp. Although I must admit, you're not quite the little scamp anymore."

Bosco smiled and said, "Do you like cartoons?"

I nodded. "Some. There were a lot of very funny ones when I was a kid. I don't quite understand the new ones though."

"I think this one is very good," Bosco said pointing at the screen. "This is one of my favorites."

So I turned to the screen and sure enough, it's one of my favorites, too.

It was about a silly old man chasing a rabbit. The rabbit would make him do all sorts of silly things which seemed embarrassing for the old guy because as a doctor, (at least that was what the rabbit called him) he seemed especially gullible. I didn't understand why a doctor

110

needed to carry a rifle and why he hadn't seen a speech therapist, but Bosco and I continued to enjoy the doctor's and rabbit's mad antics until one of the angels appeared and asked if I was ready to go. I had no idea where she was planning to take me, but I wasn't worried. I always felt safe with her.

Anyway, I replied that if she could wait until Bosco and I finished watching the cartoon, we'd been glad to go with her.

Then…

I don't know. Things got kinda crazy.

Chapter 14

"I had just gotten home from the hospital when I got Elle's call about my father," Anne said as she entered the house, carefully shrugged off her coat and dropped it on the hook behind the door. "Where's Dad now?"

Surrounded by a cloud of steam as she stood over the stove, Mrs. Tuttle jerked her thumb to Jim's bedroom as she stirred soup in a red Dutch oven pot. The smell of chicken and dumplings filled the air. "He's in there," the caregiver added. "Staring out the window. He's going to want to go out soon. He usually does this time of day. I'll feed him first then let him out in the yard."

Anne bristled and considered reprimanding Mrs. Tuttle for talking about her father as if he were a dog, but then realized Mrs. Tuttle probably didn't mean anything by it and chastised herself for focusing on such trivial matters.

"Good. You're here," Eleanor said as she breezed in from the living room. "Dr. Gerritson gave us a new medication that's been very successful in clinical trials, so there's a chance he could snap out of it in a few hours." She took a breath. "I've been called in to work for an evening conference with the company's lawyers, one of whom I'm especially interested in because of what we spoke of."

"Not a problem," Anne said, dropping her pocketbook on the kitchen table. "I'll take care of Dad when Mrs. Tuttle leaves."

Eleanor casually strode over to the pot, waved the steam into her face and inhaled. She smiled at Mrs. Tuttle. "Damn! Wish I could stay for dinner." After the caregiver nodded her appreciation, Elle turned back to Anne. "Just make sure the door to the fence remains locked from the

112

outside. With this new med, there's no telling what he'll do."

Anne nodded dispassionately. "Got it."

"Ladies," Mrs. Tuttle called over to them. "I'm bringing him to the table for dinner. Please go in the other room. You know how distracted he gets when he sees you two while he's eating."

Eleanor grabbed her coat and pocketbook. "I'm heading out anyway."

Anne pointed to her chest and then the living room, indicating she'd be camping out in there.

Slipping on her coat, Eleanor said, "I should be back before midnight. Hopefully the medication will have kicked in and Dad will be back to normal."

She gave her sister a peck on the cheek. "See you later,"

As Anne nodded, Eleanor turned, opened the door and left.

*

After dinner, me and Bosco were getting ready to leave for Whateverland when Turtledove flung open my bedroom door. "You two need to get out," she said, pointing her index finger to the hallway. "I got to clean the placc up, take out the garbage, open up some windows and air this place out. And you young fella," she said to Bosco, "don't you go lighting any matches near your grandpa's hindquarters, if he lets one fly it's likely to blow out the side of the building."

"Ha-ha," I said sarcastically. Normally I'd counter with something equally smart-mouthed, but she was cleaning up after me and since I do let one fly now and again, I let it be. Besides, we were heading out anyway, so why raise a ruckus?

113

"What part of Whaverland are we going to today Grandpa?" Bosco asked as we exited the house and made our way down the wooden deck steps.

I thought for a moment. "I believe Land o' the Midway is the ticket we'll be punching this evening, my young friend."

Bosco beamed and raised his hands with excitement. "I love Land o' the Midway! There's always so much to do!"

I patted him on the shoulder. "I'll make sure we find some fun things to pass the time," I said as I took his hand. "Hey, how did it turn out with that bully? Did you take my advice and sock him good in the breadbasket?"

Bosco O'Bama the Third nodded non-committedly as we neared the silver gates of the entrance. "We had another go-round. Everyone's telling me I fought him real good and got him on the run, but I'm not so sure. Guys like him are sneaky. Real backstabbers. Gonna keep my ears open and watch my back."

It was brave talk but I could see the concern on his face, I nodded in agreement. "That's a smart plan and one I'd stick to no matter what people say. Better safe than sorry."

We passed through the large silver gates with *Whaverland* written in cursive in an arc above, then made our way toward the Midway. The gravel crunched under our feet and the smell of popcorn and cotton candy was growing stronger, as did the sounds of the hurdy-gurdy and calliope.

As we walked down the center amid the ringing bells, flashing lights, spinning wheels of chance, the *win a prize* contests and the barkers inviting all to "See the unbelievable, the remarkable, from the furthest corners of the earth…" we spied one fellow in his late teens wearing a blue jean jacket, a red plaid flannel shirt and worn work boots approaching the **Test Your Strength** game with mallet in hand.

"Three tries for a dollar!" the straw-hatted barker shouted as onlookers gathered 'round to see if the kid had enough muscle to ring the bell and win his cutie a prize.

Rolling up his sleeves and revealing his wiry, tattooed arms, he gave a wink to his lady friend, the prerequisite wholesome 'girl-next-door' type, with her curly blond hair and dimpled cheeks, then grasped the mallet with his rough hands and raised it above his head.

BOOM! Came the sound as the mallet struck the rubber and the puck raced up the pole. After only reaching, 'Cowpoke' the puck fell and bounced a couple of times at the bottom.

As the young fellow prepared for a second try, the hurdy-gurdy music picked up and the multi-colored lights of the spinning tilt-a-whirl danced in intersecting circles across the ground. The smell of cotton candy replaced the popcorn and, as I searched for its origin, I happened to gaze upon the full moon. Floating by that white orb was a silhouette figure holding a large number of balloons.

He has to be in a harness. I thought. *No one could hold on to that many balloons for very long. His arms would give out.*

BOOM! Came the crashing sound as Flannel Shirt's second attempt rocketed up the pole. This time the black puck passed 'Cowpoke' and reached the 'Tough Guy' level before dropping. That disappointing result caused his girlfriend to pout "Aww."

"Guess your weight and age! If I can't guess your weight and age within 5 pounds or 2 years, you win a prize!" a barker called out from a nearby booth as Flannel Shirt prepared for this third attempt. He rubbed a handful of dirt across his palms, and his brows knitted in a hard look of determination.

BOOM! The air echoed as the third attempt was made. Sweat flew from Flannel Shirt's face as the mallet smashed the rubber. His girlfriend's eyes twinkled, her hands clasped in excitement as the puck raced up the pole. Up and up it went, higher, higher, almost, almost.

Then fell to earth.

Close but no cigar as the saying goes. Thems the breaks, kid.

I watched as Flannel Shirt dropped the mallet, slipped on his jean jacket and waved off the barker's attempt to get him to pony up another dollar for three more tries. I wasn't surprised at the kid's refusal. He had gone to battle to impress his fair maiden, but never made it any higher than 'Tough Guy' which really wasn't much considering there were two levels above that, Powerhouse and Superman. He had shown himself to be neither. He made it to Tough Guy however, and that title would have to suffice.

As Flannel Shirt and Girl Next Door faded into the crowd, we went over to the cotton candy booth where I bought one for Bosco and one for myself. We rode the Tilt-a-Whirl, The Rotor, The Bumper Cars and yes, no trip to Whateverland was complete without hopping aboard the mighty Whateverland Ferris Wheel with it's blue, green and yellow neon lights a'flashin' and a'blazin'.

Soon we were up in the evening air as the hurdy-gurdy below regaled us with carnival music, and while keeping

116

company with the moon and the stars, I saw the silhouette guy holding the balloons float past the moon again.

Got to be in a harness.

Unfortunately, the figure was too high and too far away for me to tell. Still, he was interesting to watch and, as the Ferris wheel kicked into gear, we did our over the tops and under the bottoms and, on Bosco's face, I saw the pure enjoyment only a kid can experience. His beaming smile made me feel good about myself, which was something I haven't felt in a long time.

As the ride drew to a close and the passengers below disembarked, I pointed out the balloon man's silhouette high above us to Bosco O'Bama the Third and said, "What do you think of that?"

Bosco peered at the full moon's balloon man imprint for quite some time. Finally he bowed his head and said, "That's so very sad."

Well, I certainly didn't see that coming!

A man floating across the evening sky upheld by a bouquet of multicolored balloons is sad?! (I assume they were multicolored, truth is I couldn't tell.) I thought he'd say, "Coooooollllll!" or "Oh, Wow! But sad? I wouldn't even have been surprised had he said "Impressive!"

I was going to ask why he thought that, but we jerked to a halt when we reached the bottom and were quickly ushered out of our seats. The carny told us to clear the area so the next group could board, and with Bosco charging ahead to select our next diversion, my question slipped through the cracks of the excitement.

The games were next. He won a stuffed dinosaur at the ring toss, lost six consecutive games of Keno, recouped at the Bowl O' Rama, and with him finally out of energy and me needing some serious down time, we chose to take a break.

As we pressed through the crowds on our way to get soda and popcorn I noticed that the single pure beam of light that ran straight into the clouds was emanating from inside the nearby Rest Area.

Hmmm. I thought. *Perhaps I could kill two birds with one stone. Rest a bit and then find out who or what is responsible for that incredible light.*

But as we neared the entrance we saw it had been roped off, with two very frightening creatures guarding the only way in. Upon closer inspection, I realized they were the soul-sucking 'Dementors' from the Harry Potter novels.

"Excuse me!" I said, calling out as I approached. "Who gave you permission to close this part of the park?"

They didn't answer, which didn't surprise me. Judging by what I'd read about them, Dementors can't talk. Nevertheless, Whateverland is my park and nothing gets closed without my say-so.

As I drew near, one Dementor raised his hand in a STOP gesture. I was going to force my way through but then his facial expression gave me pause. It was not the expected threatening glare, or aggressive confrontational stare. Instead, it was a look of warning, of caution. He even went so far as to slowly shake his head. Still, no one tells me what to do in my own park so I slipped under the rope and pressed forward. Determined to find out where that light was originating from.

Chapter 15

This certainly didn't look like any of the other Rest Areas in Whateverland. They all had picnic areas with wooden tables and barbeque grills and swings and slides and volleyball nets. All the standard family outing pleasures.

This Rest Area had rusted bulldoziers, cranes and backhoes.

It didn't take long before I realized this wasn't a Rest Area, but instead the never developed outer reaches of Whateverland.

On my right were partially dismantled buildings. But not really buildings—more like abandoned housing projects with shoddy foundations and partially constructed walls. Covered in graffiti, they featured filthy language and poorly drawn images of penises, breasts and buttocks.

On the only fully constructed wall were the words HERE, LUKE RULES! with the letters done in calligraphy. I wondered if it were done by that same kid who was bullying Bosco. Suddenly the words burst into flame but I assumed it was an illusion brought on by the reflection of the beam of light.

So I pushed on. I made my way through the mud, muck and gravel, determined to discover what that light was for.

To my surprise, each step brought an increasing sense of depression and anxiety.

Why does everything have to be so damn difficult!? I asked myself as I forced my unwilling body onward.

It was then I noticed Bosco O'Bama the Third hadn't followed me. I wasn't worried though; it was probably best that he stayed behind. After his "That's so very sad,"

119

comment, this area, with its dark aura of emptiness and worthlessness, was no place for a youngster approaching the whirlwind of puberty.

Further in, the buildings and machinery were replaced by hardscrabble brush and thickets, and I was now sure this area had *never* been open to paying customers. Just rows of large stones and leafless trees. The farther I traveled the more ominous the landscape became. Most of the trees were dead, or had fallen over, and were covered in a deep green, almost black, moss. The ground stank of rot and decay. And what bugs I could see, were big and looked like tiny robot army tanks with heavy outer shells and sharp pincers.

Lucky for me I can still see pretty good at night because I came upon a deep hole near a rectangular stone. Had I not seen it, I would have fallen in!

I stopped, took a breath, and looked around.

What in blazes am I doing out here!? Is that stupid light so important that I have to traipse through the haunted forest just to ease my childish curiosity? I'm out here alone and I'm far from being a spring chicken. What if I have a heart attack or stroke? What if I get lost? What if the Dementors prevent Bosco from coming to find me?

Cold, miserable, and depressed, I said "The hell with it!" aloud and decided to track down the shaft of light some other time.

I turned around and headed back the way I came.

I hadn't gotten far when one of the predatory bugs alit on my left arm and drove its needle like steel proboscis into it. The pain was so sharp and intense I was nearly driven to my knees. I automatically slapped at the creature and, I don't know if I got it or not, but it got *me* good. I grabbed hold of the side of a tree with my good arm to

120

steady myself and took several deep breaths until the pain subsided enough to allow me to press on.

When I finally reached the entry point to the Rest Area, I was breathing heavily and saw the Dementors were gone, so I searched the surrounding rides and games for Bosco.

The crowds had thinned and the streets held less traffic yet he was nowhere to be found. I was becoming frantic until I noticed something stir at the base of the Whateverland flagpole. Upon closer examination, I saw it was my grandson, curled into the fetal position.

I rushed over, knelt on the cold marble base and pulled him into my arms. As I placed his head against my chest, I noticed he had a bloody nose, two black eyes, and a split lip.

"What happened?" I asked, holding him in front of me so I could get a better look. He shivered as he returned my gaze with those two raccoon eyes.

"I met with a couple of my friends, and we were just talking," Bosco said in a raspy voice, "when Luke jumped me from behind. Before I could figure out what was happening, and before my friends could react, he punched me, knocked me down, and kicked me in the face and stomach. When my friends tried to grab him, he broke free and called back, 'This ain't over, Bosco. The beatings are going to get a lot worse!' My friends are still looking for him but I'm pretty sure he got away."

I pressed the boy's head against my chest once more. In the wind, the ropes of the flagpole slapped repeatedly against the metal making a clanging sound. "That little bastard," I growled, gently caressing Bosco's head as I helped him to his feet." He won't get away, I promise!"

121

Bosco continued to shiver and as he shifted his head and pressed it against my arm, the muscle just below my left shoulder roared with pain. I momentarily closed my eyes as I winced. When I reopened them…

…Jim looked around and discovered he was standing near the end of his back yard.

How did I get here? Damn it. A minute ago I was in Dr. Gerrittson's video conference room was watching a video about my…my… Damn it!… Wait… I do remember! It was a video of me skipping around like a nut in this very back yard.

Jim considered his options. When he realized he really didn't have any, at least not any with a positive outcome, his heart sank and he rose and lumbered back toward the house, cupping his still throbbing left arm.

The moon hung big and low in the sky, and as the evening wind swept across the grass, Jim looked around and tried to piece together all the things he had done while on his latest 'excursion'.

Probably doing godknowswhat out here like a flippin idiot… He shook his head in frustration when he thought of what he had seen on the video tapes. *Why can't I remember? Why does that part always draw a blank?*

As the wind again swept over the grass and rustled the nearby trees, Jim, now very tired, raised his collar and sat down on the chilly September grass and bowed his head.

"Dad?"

Startled, he looked up. Standing over him in a dark gray pants suit with a light tan knee length rawhide coat was Anne. "Are you okay?" she asked as she extended her hand. The wind blew her hair and coat back, making her

122

look like a caped superhero in silhouette. "I was watching you from the back deck and saw you suddenly sit down. Is everything all right?"

"Yeah… No… I don't know," Jim said as he took her hand, climbed to his feet, and brushed the back of his pants. "I can't explain it. It's like falling into a coma. You wake up months later with no idea what happened during the time you were unconscious."

Anne took her father's arm, gently leaned against him and walked him back to the house in the moonlight. "It must be very unsettling," she said. "Actually—horrifying."

She stopped and turned to face him, tightening her hand on his arm. "I so wish I could do something to help."

Jim saw the hurt, concern, fear, and just about every other soul-wrenching emotion in every small line on her face as the ghost of that three-year-old girl with the green sparkling eyes superimposed itself. That trusting little girl who told him he made her feel safe. And as he continued to gaze into her eyes, he saw the same desperate helplessness he himself felt those many years ago.

Daddy, please help me!

And that look tore at old wounds because Jim knew the horror of being completely helpless while your loved one suffered.

What was worse was that this horror—the one he was putting his daughters through—apparently had no end. At least when Anne had the flu, the worst was over in a single night. A single night that left a scar on Jim's psyche that he would carry to his grave.

How bad is the scarring I'm leaving on my daughters? How long will they be forced to carry it?

As they neared the house, Anne placed her head on Jim's shoulder. As his mind continued to clear, he asked, "How are *you* feeling? How are your ribs?"

Anne raised her head, looked at him, and gave a dismissive shrug. "I'm on the mend. I'm relatively young, have great genes and my old man's stubborn refusal to let a couple of cracked bones get in my way."

"Yeah, you're your father's daughter all right!" Jim said beaming. Both his daughters not only closely resembled him physically, they also had his personality. He remembered once jokingly asking his ex-wife if she was sure Anne, Eleanor, and Bob were actually her children.

It was supposed to be a funny. Barbara had natural childbirth for all three so there was never any doubt, but Barbara hadn't laughed. At times she seemed upset that none of her children—not even her daughters—looked or acted anything like her. Barbara had straight black hair, Anne was blond, Eleanor had sandy brown, and Bob reddish maroon. Barbara had olive-colored skin and brown eyes, traits none of her three children carried.

As they drew closer to the house Jim wondered if that lack of similarity was a factor in Barbara's decision to leave. Maybe as the years passed and her children's resemblance to their father increased, she felt more like a surrogate. Maybe that's what made it possible for her to empty their bank accounts and turn her back on her family.

As they climbed the stairs to the back deck, Jim decided it wasn't a topic worth dwelling upon.

What's past is past and its gas, grass or ass 'cause nobody rides for free. So get out of my head, Barbara, your lease is up and it's time you hit the road. And having come to that decision, Jim felt content.

124

Anne saw this and her face brightened. "Well, look at that!" she said as she turned at the top of the deck stairs to face him under the bright lights. "Is that a smile?" She took a step toward him and eyed him with a wide grin.

He smelled liquor on her breath and thought that was NOT a good idea as she was on pain medication. She reached up and placed her fingers and thumbs on either side of his face and squeezed. "I just love it when you smile. I… Hey," she said as she dropped her hand and took a step back. "Where did Mr. Smile go?"

Mr. Smile was indeed gone, and the Jim she knew as a child, the man she and her sister would jokingly refer to as "He Who Would Take No Shit!" was now standing before her.

He gently placed his hands on either side of her shoulders and said, "Honey, you shouldn't be drinking while you're on pain medication."

Here expression immediately changed. "That never stopped you!?" she shot back with such venom that he wondered, (and dreaded) what he might have said or done while off on one of his 'excursions', to warrant such an attack.

He kept his hands on her upper arms, holding them casually but firmly. The trees rustled and moonlight beamed across the extensive expanse of the back yard.

He eyed her carefully. "I don't remember EVER taking medication while you girls and your brother were growing up. I don't remember ever being sick."

Anne's eyes welled up and he slightly loosened his grip. She bowed her head. "You're right," she said. Jim released her as she turned and walked slowly to the wooden fence that enclosed their back deck. "I'm sorry I lashed out."

125

Jim came over and tilted his head so he could see her eyes. "You've been through a life-threatening experience. Often times people need counseling and therapy to deal with…"

She shook her head. "It's not that. Well… maybe that's part of it, but that isn't what's bothering me." She paused momentarily, then said, "I'm questioning my decision to become a police officer."

That comment stunned Jim, and he needed a moment to process it. This was new territory. Over the years he often referred to Anne as his Vulcan child because she had Mr. Spock's highly disciplined and logical mind. Jim couldn't think of a single instance where his Vulcan child hadn't meticulously assessed her situation and comprised a logical solution. Once done, her decisions were never questioned. Yes, this was indeed new territory.

He directed her to the left cedar bench. There were two. Each straddled the back door and Jim and Anne sat side by side beneath the wrought iron lamps. He placed his arm around her and held her tight.

"All right," he said, extending his legs and crossing his ankles. "You have my attention. And… since I appear to have all my facilities for the time being," he said with a couple of gentle taps to her hand, "tell me what the problem is."

When he looked at her the way every loving father looks at his daughter, with that amazed look that tells her how astonished he is that someone as beautiful and wonderful as she could be his child, and saw him powering up to go into yet another battle on her behalf, to protect her from whatever upset her, from whatever hurt her.

She felt safe, and protected …

126

… like a little girl.

She gazed into his eyes and noticed his dilated pupils, a side-effect of the medication. Seeing this, her heart sank and realized that as much as she wanted his input, she couldn't accept it, because the brain behind those wide pupils was as fragile as a robin's egg.

"To be honest, Dad, I think I would prefer just sitting here with you, looking out into the night."

He eyed her again. "You sure you don't want to talk about it?" He specifically used a tone fashioned to console her and coax her to 'just let it out.'

But as he said earlier, she was her father's daughter and could no more hurt him than he could hurt her.

"Nope," she said with a quick smile. She took his arm, pulled it across her shoulder and snuggled closer to him. The fringes from her rawhide coat lined up along his thigh. " I just want to sit here with you and look at the moon."

He smiled as they both sat back, but as they did, Jim thought he saw something in that growing night sky. Something sailing by.

A hot-air balloon? he thought, then dismissed the idea.

They stayed on the front deck for another fifteen-minutes, only to come inside when Jim's watch beeped indicating it was time to take another pill.

Once inside, Jim took his meds. By 8:30 he was in bed and fast asleep, completely unaware of the terrors to come.

Chapter 16

Eleanor arrived home shortly before midnight. She looked a little bedraggled and headed straight for the wine cabinet in the living room after hanging her coat on the hook and dropping her pocketbook on the kitchen table.

"Dad in bed?" she asked as she passed Anne, who was sitting on the couch reading a dog-eared paperback version of *How to Win Friends and Influence People* by Dr. Norman Vincent Peale. Elle opened the wine cabinet door, looked around a bit and pulled out a bottle.

Anne closed the book and replied, "Yep. In bed and asleep, I just checked on him."

"Got some good news," Eleanor said, quickly uncorking a bottle of merlot and pouring its contents into her glass. "I got you a lawyer!" Once done, she put down the bottle and raised her glass in a toast. "And not just a regular lawyer, my dear—I managed to retain the services of Scott Tremaine, Esquire, who, let me tell you, is one of the sharpest and most-feared attorneys in the whole USA." Eleanor took a sip then smiled from ear to ear. "In addition to being a real hunka, hunka, burnin' love. Wink, wink."

Anne eyed her. The lampshade she had tilted to provide better lighting for her book was now making her appear stern and matronly. "Elle that's wonderful, but what's this going to cost me? Lawyers that good don't come cheap."

Eleanor strode over, plopped into the cavernous brown leather living room recliner and kicked off her shoes. "Funny you should ask," she commented just before taking another sip. "As it turned out, price isn't an issue."

128

Anne smirked, put her book on the coffee table and turned to Eleanor as her sister leaned back and the attached ottoman rose, lifting her feet.

"Yep, not even a consideration," Eleanor said, snuggling into a fully relaxed position. She then placed her elbow on the chair arm and leaned in conspiratorially to Anne. "And would you like to know why?"

Anne stared suspiciously, "I'm not sure. Would I?"

Eleanor grinned, her face brightening. "Oh yes, indeed you would!" She took another swallow, let out a contented sigh and wiggled her feet in excitement.

"Well then," Anne said, folding her hands in front of her, "let's have it."

Elle sat up excitedly, quickly finished her wine and said, "Turns out two things fell right into place. One, Goldenrod is in the process of purchasing the Great Experience Cruise Lines—that's why I was summoned to that meeting tonight. Oh and in case you're wondering, I was given a promotion *and* the job of bringing Great Experience into the Goldenrod family. So I'll be the boss—plus I've dealt with these things before and believe me, the negotiations are going to be brutal. Tremaine very much wants to lead the transition team so I let him know that I just may be persuaded to let him do just that— after I find a top notch lawyer to defend my sister in a civil case."

"Oh, Elle," Anne said, pressing her fingers to her face in disapproval. "You can't do that. It's unprofessional and probably illegal. It wouldn't be right."

Eleanor grinned, leaned over and patted Anne on the knee. "Aww, how sweet! You really don't have any idea how the business world works now do you?"

129

Before Anne could respond, Eleanor leapt from the recliner with glass in hand, sauntered to the wine cabinet and added, "Now, as for the second piece that fell into place. Ol' Scotty boy comes from a cop family. His father was a New York City detective, and his brother is in the FBI. And when I told him what happened, he was genuinely pissed off and nearly begged me to let him take your case. Promised me he'd have it thrown out before week's end and that he'd do it gratis."

Anne's jaw dropped as she stood. "That's unbelievable, Elle!" But as Anne took a step, she suddenly stopped. Her expression changed, and she eyed her kid sister suspiciously. "You're not trying to blow one by me are you? You know how tenacious I am. I *will* find out if you're picking up the tab."

Eleanor's smile disappeared. She placed her glass on top of the wine cabinet, put her hands on her hips and scowled. "What the hell is wrong with you?! I just brought you the best news possible and you accuse me of manipulating things behind your back?!" She stepped forward with a facial expression that made it clear that if Anne wanted a fight, she was going to get a doozy.

"Sorry! Sorry!" Anne said. She returned to the couch and sat down. "I'm just going through a rough patch. I'm questioning the choices I've made, and the more I look, the more it seems I've been heading in the wrong direction. Anyway," she said, as her countenance transformed into a more cheerful one, "congratulations on the promotion. You're barely in your thirties and already in line to run a major corporation. Good for you!"

Eleanor dropped the confrontational stance, picked up her wine and returned to the recliner. "Actually, there is a downside to this whole merger thing," she said as she sat.

She was about to place the glass on the end table, but instead, brought it to her lips and downed the entire glassful in several rapid swallows.

Anne gave her a sideways glance. "And that downside is...?

"Well," Eleanor said, placing the empty glass on the table. "Great Experience's headquarters is in Manhattan. Elliot has decided buy their Great X building, keep their operation there and within a few years transfer Goldenrod's Headquarters there, too." While speaking, Eleanor drew a cigarette from her purse, lit it, and exhaled a plume of smoke. "Says if we're going to be competing with the major hotel chains, it's time for us to make our presence known in the Big Apple."

Anne folded her hands. "So you'll be moving to Manhattan once the merger is completed?"

Eleanor took a quick drag, then brushed at a piece of ash that dropped on her slacks. "Looks that way, yeah."

Anne rose, walked over to the wine cabinet, and poured herself a glass from the already opened bottle.

"Hey!" Eleanor called out. "You shouldn't be drinking while taking pain meds. You've seen enough junkie OD's to know how that combo turns out."

Anne picked up her glass and took a sip. "The meds wore off hours ago. Besides, wine relaxes me." She picked up the bottle and brought it and her glass over to the couch, placed them on the end table, and sat down. "I can handle the pain. So, when are you moving to Manhattan?"

With her elbow on the armrest, Elle placed her hand on her chin. "Not for a while yet. Definitely not before spring. The transition is expected to be complete shortly after the New Year so I'll be spending a lot of time between now and then traveling back and forth." She

131

suddenly looked at her cigarette with an expression of 'what-the-hell-am-I-doing?' and crushed it in the ashtray. She turned and studied Anne.

"So, you're reevaluating your choices, huh?" she said. "Never expected that from you, Little Miss I-have-a-detailed-life-plan-that-will-ensure-my-future-health-and-financial-well-being... type... person." Eleanor chuckled, "Didn't quite know how to end that one. Anyway what brought this on?"

Anne eyed her sister sideways. "Really? You need to ask? After all that's happened?"

Eleanor shrugged. "Well, it's just that it's coming from YOU, the most self-assured person I've ever known. What was it Dad used to call you? His little... space-something?"

Anne grinned and tucked her feet up under her on the couch. "His little Vulcan child. Yeah, the thing is, when you make those plans you don't factor in the reality because you only know what you've been told, not how crazy the job really is or how split-second decisions affect you."

Eleanor gave a quick nod. "I suppose I'm learning that, too. I never thought I'd move out of this area, but I'm ambitious and want to play with the big kids." She sighed, looked away and drummed her fingers on the base of her wine glass. "Should have realized that would take me out of my comfort zone. It's disheartening, I suppose, but that's part of life, right? What's that old saying? If you want to make God laugh, tell Him your plans?"

Just then, an ear-splitting howl of terror exploded from their father's bedroom.

132

Chapter 17

The blinds were up as Jim placed his hands on the sides of the window and stared out into the night. The room was pitted by a collection of sharp angles in various moonlit shades of gray. The bright shaft of light shone in the distance, beaming into the sky from the furthest reaches of Whateverland.

Next time, I will go all the way. I will find where that light is coming from.

But he felt a sudden chill as he recounted his foray into that desolate area. The rancid smells, the bizarre bugs, the rocks that jutted out of the ground like broken fingers.

It's a bad place.

But then he recalled Bosco O'Bama the Third calling to him from that very area. *I'm here, I'm always here, and you'll never have to worry about me again,* the boy had said, which made matters even more confusing. If the boy was familiar with the area, why didn't he accompany him when he pushed past the Dementors and headed toward the light?

And what about that bizarre comment he made about the balloon man? What could he possibly find sad about that?

Clouds gathered and paled the moonlight. Whateverland, now closed for the night, took on an eerie ghost town appearance as flattened popcorn boxes and cotton candy tubes, propelled by the wind, skipped along the rides and carnival games of the Midway.

That's when Jim realized everything was in black and white. His room, the sky, the ride in Whateverland. It was as if all color had been removed from the world.

Except for one lone object.

133

In the distance brightly colored balloons, clustered together, above a silhouetted figure gently soared through the night sky. The balloons weren't merely colored, they were dazzling! They were more like orbs of assorted bright neon. Radiant blue, shocking pink, sunshine yellow, jade green, all as vibrant and alive as the lights of Las Vegas!

That's so very sad, the boy had said.

His thoughts were interrupted when the balloons began pulsing and throbbing. Various sections of the balloons would light, then darken, only to be immediately replaced by others with different colors, like fireworks on the Fourth of July.

He almost applauded.

The balloons drifted closer and became even more vibrant, more colorful. His walls were filled with bursts of radiant, flashing light.

Still, an ominous feeling enveloped him.

The balloons continued to draw nearer with seemingly endless displays of startling color combinations.

The feeling of dread steadily increased.

The flashing lights allowed him to see the figure beneath the balloons. Strangely, the person was back on, and the balloons themselves blocked Jim's view of the man's upper torso. The figure wore a dark suit, with well-tailored pants, and brightly polished black shoes that reflected the light show.

The figure with the balloons drew ever closer, and Jim was eager to see just who had been sailing around that entire evening. The balloons slowly gave a quarter turn bringing the figure's right arm into view.

Like the left, it hung limply by his side.

But how...? Where is the...?

134

Another quarter turn and the mystery unfolded.

The man's head was bowed and his face was ashen grey. Below the chin, tightly wrapped around his throat, were the strings from the balloons, wound and bulging like those on a kite string spindle.

As Jim shook, the dead feet of the figure tapped just below the window sill. Suddenly all the balloons lit up, exposing the figure's face.

A face Jim immediately recognized.

No, no, it cannot be. It cannot be...

The figure's eyes opened. The mouth moved.

"Why didn't you visit me at the hospital, Jimmy boy?" the figure growled with hatred. "Why didn't you visit your old Dad?"

The terror that had been building had finally found its voice.

Chapter 18

When the girls burst into the room, Jim, having just awakened from a terribly frightening dream, jerked into a sitting position in his bed with his pajama top covered in sweat, his arms waving and his eyes wide with terror.

"Wha... Wha... What?" His eyes darted around as Anne snapped on the overhead light. His heart beat with an odd rhythm, quieting as the sense of danger passed.

Eleanor ran over to the bed and knelt beside her terrified father. "Dad, are you all right? What happened?"

Jim pressed his hand to his head then scooted back against the wooden headboard. "I had a dream, I... think. I'm not sure. It was all so confusing. I dreamed I was standing at the window," as he spoke, he pointed to the window to his right.

The blinds were pulled to the top, which Anne thought unusual because Mrs. Tuttle usually lowered and closed them while Jim ate dinner. Anne now wondered if the blinds were up when she checked on him earlier.

She couldn't remember. *That's it! I'm done with those damn meds!*

"I was at a circus," Jim began and then stopped. His expression indicating he was unsure if what he was saying was accurate. "It really wasn't a circus," he continued as he rubbed his forehead. "I remember this guy with balloons. And there was something wrong with him, something that bothered me, but I... I'm..." He lowered his hand to the side of his face in frustration. "I... can't... I don't seem..." He let out a heavy sigh. "I'm sorry, girls. Sorry if I upset you. Probably just a bad dream. It seemed so real, though." He raked his hand across his chin. "I'm all right now. You can go back inside."

136

Eleanor took his hand. "Are you sure? I can stay till you fall asleep."

Jim smiled and patted the back of her hand. "Thanks, honey, but I'll be all right. Like I said, it's probably just a bad dream brought on by all the craziness we've been dealing with lately or maybe the new meds or…" He shrugged. "…just my body's way of dealing with the stress."

As Eleanor stood and Anne snapped off the light, Anne, now in silhouette said, "If you need anything, just let us know. We'll be spending the next few nights in our old rooms."

Jim was suddenly very sleepy and slid back down into the covers. "Okay, girls, thank you. We'll talk in the morning."

As Eleanor followed the hall light to the door, she took one last look back at the frail and confused old man sleeping in her father's bed and was suddenly shaken by the thought that perhaps what she saw tonight was the opening scene of her father's final chapter.

The next morning, Jim made his way through the kitchen on his way to the bathroom. Mrs. Tuttle was at the stove,cooking and turned to him as he passed. "What do you want for breakfast? I can tell you what we have if you've forgotten."

Jim shook his head. "Just coffee and a muffin. Let me know when it's ready. I'll bring it out on the deck."

She nodded and opened the cupboard doors for the coffee and coffee cups.

After Jim finished with the bathroom and entered the kitchen, he checked his watch. "Have the girls left?"

137

"Eleanor has," Mrs. Tuttle replied as she placed the cups on the countertop. "Anne's still sleeping."

Jim nodded, remembering his eldest was on disability leave and thought it good she was getting the extra rest.

"Your pills are on the table," Mrs. Tuttle said as she ladled the coffee into the machine.

Jim nodded, grabbed a small box of orange juice from the refrigerator, peeled it open and took a seat at the table. He eyed the pills and said, "Okay, here goes," and he took each pill with a sip of orange juice until gone.

Jim grimaced, "I hate the aftertaste of those damn things. No matter how fast I swallow, I always get that medicinal backwash. Damn near makes me gag."

Just as he finished speaking, Mrs. Tuttle placed a bran muffin on a mid-sized saucer in front of him. "Take a couple small bites and chew slowly," she said as she dried her hands on her apron. "That should clear your palette and get rid of the aftertaste."

He did as suggested and by the third bite, the medicinal taste was gone.

When the coffee was served, he placed his cup alongside the muffin on the saucer and walked out to the back deck. Once settled on the bench, he placed the saucer beside him, sipped his coffee and stared into the back yard.

Fifteen minutes later the back door opened and Anne, still dressed in her light blue pajamas and with coffee in hand, stepped onto the deck and took a seat beside her father.

Shortly afterward Mrs. Tuttle poked her head out and announced she was leaving to do the week's shopping. "Do you need anything not on the list?"

Anne thought for a moment and shook her head. "I can't think of anything. How long do you think you'll be?

Mrs. Tuttle thought for a moment. "No more than an hour and a half," she replied. "I've pretty much got this down to a science."

After Mrs. Tuttle left, Jim watched as Anne got up and leisurely strolled the deck. "Beautiful day, isn't it?" she asked, placing her coffee cup on the railing and raising her head. She looked at the perfect blue sky and the fluffy white clouds in an especially pleasant sunlit morning. Her blond hair fluttered in the light breeze.

Jim smiled. "Oh, that it is!" he replied. He pulled back, tilted his head to the side and studied his daughter's profile. "You're getting your color back, and the dark lines under your eyes are gone. Looks like you're on the road to a full recovery."

She continued gazing into the back yard. "Feeling better," she said, turning toward him. "I was thinking about taking a ride in the country. Do a little leaf peeping, maybe hit one of those apple orchards and pick up a box of cider donuts." She smiled as she reached for her cup and took a sip. "Man, could I go for one of those right now! Don't you just love those things dunked in hot java on a crisp September morning?"

Jim nodded. "I do. And I think you getting out in the sun and driving around is a great idea. But before you go, I need you to tell me what happened to my car, my keys, my wallet and charge cards? I know I own a bright yellow Mustang ragtop but it's not in the driveway or the garage. I've scoured my room and can't find any of my personal things, like my checkbook, driver's license, tax records, you know what I'm talking about. There must be a reason why they're gone and I'd like to know why."

It was unsettlingly eerie that as those words left his mouth, the sun slipped behind the clouds, Anne's cheery mood disappeared and her sallow pallor returned.

It pained him that his questions were upsetting her, but he was a man without an identity and needed answers. Jim added, "I hate putting you on the spot and believe me, I would much prefer to hash this out with Eleanor, but she's busy with work and you're here right now so, let's get this over with. I need to know where I stand."

Anne drained her cup, placed it on the bench next to the saucer, then sat on the deck railing in front of her father. She folded her arms and with tight-lipped determination said, "Elle and I sold your car, cancelled your credit cards, removed all the money from your bank account, cashed in your stocks, and had the courts award us ownership of this house."

Visibly stunned, Jim said, "Why would you…"

Anne held up her hand and said quite forcibly, "Stop! You need to listen. I'll answer all your questions, but first you have to hear the whole story. Deal?"

Jim huffed, leaned back and folded his arms. With lips pressed together, he spit out the word, "Deal."

Anne nodded, took a moment then stood and began pacing, "Your condition didn't happen overnight. It took several weeks before Eleanor and I realized something was wrong. It started when Elle and I started getting complaints from the neighbors. They said you were regularly walking around the front yard in your underwear and had urinated into the flowerbed in broad daylight."

Anne bit down on her lip, turned away and looked into the distance. Her eyes glistened with tears. She forced

140

herself to continue. "I heard from friends on the force that several complaints had been filed against you."

She studied the deck floor, determined not to eye him as she spoke. "I won't go into detail but the reports regarding your behavior were disturbing. Eleanor and I took turns stopping by, you know, to make sure you were okay. And as it happened, every time we did visit, you were fine. We'd chat, have dinner, and go for a walk. All normal. Eleanor said the same thing, so I started to suspect that the neighbors, for whatever reason, had it in for you."

She took another breath and resumed pacing. "Then one day, I stopped by, and while in the kitchen, I heard a commotion coming from the front of the house. People were yelling, car horns were blowing and I wondered what the hell was going on.

"I looked outside and didn't see anything unusual, but then saw Mrs. Harding pointing at you. You were standing on the other side of your car in the driveway. You seemed fine, a little red-faced perhaps and were apparently oblivious to whatever concern the woman had. So I rushed out to see why our neighbors were pointing."

Jim's face had turned grim. "I assume that's the time I was urinating on the side of my car, thinking I was washing it?"

She didn't immediately reply. After a few moments, she said, "That was the *first* time I saw you do that."

Jim bowed his head, closed his eyes, and sighed deeply. "Oh dear Lord! Oh, Anne I am so sorry! I would never embarrass you intentionally. I would never..."

She held up her hand. "Stop, Dad! This isn't easy and there's a lot more I have to say. Just let me say it, and then we'll talk."

141

Jim took a breath, nodded and lowered his head in shame.

Anne continued. "When I realized you had no idea what you were doing I called an ambulance. You kicked and screamed and had developed such a high temperature that your hallucinations led you to believe you were being attacked. The police were called and you had to be restrained and sedated by the EMT's before we finally got you to go.

Fortunately, Dr. Gerritson was performing surgery at the hospital that day and when asked to examine you, ran a few tests and within hours diagnosed your condition as a viral brain infection. A very virulent one, and one resistant to most medications and treatments.

"When Elle and I were told the bad news, they suggested we place you in hospice because there is no known treatment. We refused and instead brought you to several specialists, all of whom confirmed Dr. Gerrittson's diagnosis."

With an expression of bitter resolve, Anne took a seat next to Jim on the bench and gently placed her hand on his knee. "We sold your car and other belongings because, when on your excursions, you are incapable of knowing or understanding what you're doing. You know what I'm saying is true because you've seen the videos.

"We had your driver's license cancelled, as well as your credit cards. Face it, Dad. Could you ever look at yourself in the mirror if you had run over someone while in your fugue state? Or emptied your bank account or maxed out your credit cards on some telemarketing scam or signed over your royalties from Bob's app business?"

His first reaction was to argue with her. How dare she think of him like that!

142

But…

…she was right. Things had changed dramatically and he had no idea how much difficulty he put his daughters through over the last year, so he held his tongue and motioned for her to continue.

She held up her hands with fingers splayed, "I'm sorry, I'm sorry," she said, shaking her head. "I'm a little on edge." She slowly drew a breath. "Anyway, we petitioned the court to take full control of your affairs." She shoved her hands into the pockets of her pajamas, rose and began pacing. "After Dr. Gerrittson testified and showed the judge the videos, Eleanor and I were jointly awarded power of attorney and full control over your estate, with the provision that all monies collected from the sale or dispersement of your wealth and property be put into a special account that would only be used for your benefit, medical care and…" She was about to say funeral expenses, but changed direction, "… other expenses."

"So there you have it," Anne said as she stopped in front of him. "We have a court approved lawyer/accountant in charge of your liquid assets. I can show it to you online. It's all there. All the income from the sales and all the expenses for your care. Would you like to have a look?"

Jim thought for a moment and shook his head. "Maybe some other time."

When she took a seat beside him, he took her hand in his. "Honey, it's time to put an end to this. You and your sister should be enjoying your lives. I could understand if there was a possibility that I might get better, but that's not going to happen."

"Dad, there's always hope! Each day they discover new…"

143

This time it was Jim who held up his hand. "Stop!" he said. "This time you listen. I appreciate all you and your sis...

Suddenly, Jim stood, grabbed his stomach and bent over. He took a quick glance at the backdoor, shook his head, then leapt toward the deck railing. A moment later, he was vomiting.

Chapter 19

Jim vomited several times over the next twenty minutes, mostly on the bushes nearest the deck railing. When it finally stopped, Anne led him inside and eased him into a seat in the kitchen near the bathroom.

Anne used the wall phone to call the doctor's office. Moments later she said, "Dr. Gerritson said vomiting may be a side effect of the medication." She didn't mention that he ALSO said vomiting may indicate a further deterioration of Jim's condition. She then added, "If the vomiting continues for more than an hour, he wants you to come straight in."

With his stomach calming, Jim cautiously rose, walked to the sink, filled a tumbler with water and slowly drank it.

"Easy, Dad," Anne cautioned, "you don't want to start hurling again."

He waved her off. "I'm okay now. Just need to get that sick taste out of my mouth." He placed his left hand on the sink rim to steady himself and took long deep breaths.

After placing the tumbler in the sink, he turned to her and said. "I meant what I said out there. If this..." he gestured to the back deck and the sink, "... is a harbinger of what's to come, then I don't see where you and Elle have any choice."

Anne shook her head determinedly. "We don't know if this is an easily corrected side- effect or something more serious. What Eleanor and I have learned over the last year is not to make assumptions regarding your condition, good or bad. We wait for clinical information and medical evidence. If this new medication is as effective as the clinical trials suggest, then we might see some real improvement."

145

Jim wasn't buying it. As he washed out the glass and placed it in the dish rack he said, "Be realistic, hon. I've seen the videos. I'm too far gone to beat this thing." He slid his hands into his pockets, walked over and looked out the kitchen door window.

Anne approached and gently placed her hand on his back. "I remember a man once saying, 'I don't care what it costs in time, money or well-being. I will not rest, I will not stop, I will not give an inch. I will fight this thing with every breath, with every heartbeat, and with every fiber of my being until we win.'"

Jim turned from the window and eyed her. She was quoting his exact words, said after arriving home from the hospital after Bob had suddenly relapsed one afternoon and grew critically ill in a matter of hours. And Jim was true to his word—he hadn't given up and somehow Bob lived an additional six months.

When Mrs. Tuttle returned from the supermarket, she placed the items on the counter and noticed Jim's room door was closed. Since it was routinely left open when Jim wasn't in it, she became curious. When she heard one of the back deck floorboards creak and the sound of water running, she went to investigate.

Looking out the back door window, she saw Anne spraying the shrubs and stairs with the garden hose.

When Anne heard the back door open, she turned and said, "Ah, Mrs. Tuttle, you're back."

The caregiver stepped onto the deck. "Got everything on the list, plus a plastic mattress cover. Since your dad's condition is steadily deteriorating, it might come in handy should he…" She sniffed. "What's that smell?" She waved

146

her hand in front of her face. "Did someone vomit? Has your father…?"

Anne released the hose trigger and said, "Yeah, Dad had a reaction to the new meds." Dragging the hose behind her, she walked down the stairs and over to the line of shrubs. "I'm wondering if the medication might be more damaging than the disease itself."

With a concerned look, Mrs. Tuttle walked down and joined Anne. "You and your sister can only make decisions based on the information the doctors give you. That's all you can do."

As Anne sprayed the shrubs her expression became solemn. "I just need to be sure that whatever decisions I make doesn't wind up hurting him."

"Anne," Mrs. Tuttle said as she placed a comforting hand on her shoulder. "Judging from my experience, you're not always given that option." She shot a look to the house. "Where's your father now?"

"The vomiting tired him out, so I suggested he lie down and rest."

Mrs. Tuttle took the hose from Anne and said, "You're still recovering yourself. Go inside. I'll finish cleaning this mess."

147

Chapter 20

As Jim lay on his bed, he rubbed his stomach. It hurt and he was concerned that if his body was resisting the new meds, and he continued to vomit, he would be spending more time in that whateverland he disappeared into.

He suddenly found himself questioning if that were still true. Some of the things and events were falling into place, at least judging by the videos he had seen.

In them, he appeared to be in a place where there were horses, fishing, sailing, and rides of some sort, (that was the impression he got when he saw himself raising his arms and shortly after, grabbing onto an imaginary bar and pulling back as if experiencing g-forces.)

Then there was food and drink. And the invisible child companion.

And finally the Door That Separated Everything.

There are two places, he suddenly realized. *One place where my movements and reactions are those of a person doing ordinary things, like watching TV, listening to music, or reading a book. But then, there was that pantomime of me pulling open a large door that led to the place where all the crazy things happen.*

Wait, what crazy things? What...What was I thinking? It was... it was...

"Whatcha doin', Pop-Pop?" Bosco O'Bama the Third asked. Startled, I spun around and noticed the boy eyeing me and then scrunch up his nose. "You smell kinda funky." He said as he grabbed a chair, pulled it over to the side of my bed and sat.

148

I nodded and grimaced a bit. "I expect I do. I've been sick. My stomach hurts."

Just then the door opened and Cap'n Spaulding entered with Polly on his shoulder wearing a tiny sombrero. "Ahoy, matey!" the Cap'n said. "What's this I hear about you feeling poorly?"

"Pop-Pop's just under the weather, that's all. No big deal," Bosco O'Bama the Third quickly replied.

Polly perked up and said "NFW!" with real concern.

Bosco nodded. "Yeah, way. How about you?"

"SSDD." the parrot replied.

The Cap'n pulled his pocket watch, checked the time, shook his head, pulled over a chair across from Bosco and with a friendly smile said, "Well, there's nothing better to cure your ills than taking a sail out over the bounding main." He raised his hand and gestured to the sunlit window. "It's beautiful day for it."

It was a beautiful day but I immediately dismissing the idea of going anywhere. "Normally I'd agree but my stomach's dead set against it." I said as I felt a twinge and hoped it wasn't signaling another session of kneeling over the porcelain throne.

With a disappointed look the Cap'n said, "Well, okay. But sooner or later we're going to have to take that sail and judging by the way you look, I'd say the sooner the better."

I sat up. "Wait! What do you mean by sooner or later I'll HAVE to take that sail?"

The Cap'n stood and was about to reply when Polly flapped his wings wildly and shouted "STFU! STFU!"

The Cap'n turned to the bird, slowly nodded, then ran his hand down his face and sighed in disappointment. "My apologies," he said. "My tongue got away from me." He

149

picked up the chair and returned it to its place against the wall. "May you have a quick recovery."

As he headed toward the door he glared at Bosco. "A word, lad," he said.

As he and Bosco walked to the far side of the room, I was able to overhear much of their conversation even though they spoke in hushed tones. The trouble was the meds made it so I couldn't quite make sense out of what they were saying.

"You're not helping him, you know," I heard the Cap'n whisper. "And frankly, I'm here as much for you as I am for him."

"True," Bosco said shooting a glance at me. "But I've already taken that sail and know what to expect. He doesn't and deserves the time necessary to put the pieces together. You can't deny he's owed that."

Polly bobbed his head up and down. "Tru dat!"

The Cap'n eyed the bird. "Hush, you. We've business here." He turned back to Bosco. "Do you really want to go through this again? Wasn't the first time difficult enough? I mean look at you, you're clearly suffering."

Bosco paled a little. "Just a little more time," he finally said. "He's done this for his loved ones. It's only fair that he reap what he sowed."

The Cap'n lowered his head. "Aye and noted, lad. But be advised, the longer you delay the more likely I'll have to force the issue, like I did with you. And neither of us wants that."

The Cap'n's words struck a chord and Bosco nodded solemnly. "I understand the complexities involved and mean you no ill will. I simply need just a little more time to fully prepare."

150

Realizing there was nothing more to be said, the Cap'n nodded, turned, and headed toward the door.

"L8TR PPL" Polly said with a tip of his tiny sombrero.

I don't remember anything after that. I guess I fell asleep.

It was about an hour later when I awoke. I looked around, sat up and swung my legs over to the floor. Then saw Bosco sitting on the far end of the bed reading a comic book. "You're looking a little pale, young fella," I said, "still having trouble with that Luke kid?"

Bosco didn't answer right away. His face just hung there, expressionless. Finally he bowed his head and said. "It's like he's stalking me. No matter where I go or what I do I get the feeling he's hiding nearby just waiting for the chance to beat me up."

This had gone far enough. "Your mother and I are going over to the school to have a talk with the principal. This Luke sounds like a psycho. And you gotta be real careful with that type. You get in their crosshairs and you could wind up dead."

Just then someone banged on the door.

"Who is it!?"

"It's me!" Turtledove called back. "Who the hell else would it be?"

With a sigh I rose from the bed and felt a twinge in my stomach. After taking a breath I cautiously walked over and opened the door.

She stormed in, dressed in full SWAT team gear. She was about to speak when I decided it was more important to address this Luke situation first. "Turtledove, you're just the person I wanted to talk to." I said as I closed the door behind her. "Bosco's having trouble with a bully at

151

school and I want it stopped. Why the boy's all upset and I…"

Mrs. Tuttle pulled back, shook her head and said, "Oh, not this Bosco thing again. Look Mr. August, you're confused. There is no Bosco and I don't have a son!"

"What?! You can't be serious! And… and… and why are you calling me Mr. August?"

As Mrs. Tuttle exhaled in exasperation, I started to panic, "For heaven's sake, Bosco," I called out, "tell your mother who you are?"

When I received no answer, I spun around and discovered Bosco wasn't there, and the chair he had been sitting in was back against the wall.

*

"…then with a look of total bewilderment he crawled back into bed. He's been asleep ever since." Mrs. Tuttle shrugged. "Do either of you have any idea who this Bosco Obama the Third is? Could he have been a friend from childhood? Although considering how unusual the name is, that's highly unlikely. Maybe it has something to do with the former president?"

Anne, Eleanor and Mrs. Tuttle were all sitting at the kitchen table having dinner. Mrs. Tuttle usually ate with Jim, but he skipped tonight's meal, and so she joined the daughters for a repast of soup, salad, and roast chicken. It was early evening and Eleanor had just arrived home from work only minutes earlier and had asked to be caught up on the day's events.

Anne shook her head in response to Mrs. Tuttle's question. "Also unlikely. Dad stopped following politics ages ago. Said they were all crooks and he wanted no part of it."

152

Eleanor pressed her lips together and stabbed at the remaining pieces of lettuce, tomato and red onion on her plate. "Frankly, I don't have a clue," she said. "Although he has mentioned this Bosco character before. He was skipping around in the backyard—when Anne and I approached. We were chatting when Dad suddenly became fearful and started looking around in panic, saying things like... well I don't remember his exact words but it was something like, 'I need Bosco. Or, I've got to get Bosco.' We thought he was talking about that chocolate drink, so we went back to the house and made him a cup of hot cocoa."

With a just-my-luck shake of her head, Anne said, "Damnedest thing is I left the house just five minutes earlier or I could have seen it for myself. Maybe ask questions about his past that might reveal who he's talking about."

"Why? Where did you go?" Eleanor asked as she ransacked her pocketbook for her Nicorette gum.

"I went for a ride. Did a little leaf peeping," Anne replied. "I just wanted to get away from all the craziness for a little while." She chuckled sarcastically. "And when I returned, good ol' craziness was waiting patiently at the door holding a moose turd pie fresh from the oven!"

As Eleanor pulled a strip of Nicorette gum from her purse and placed her hand on Anne's shoulder to reassure her, Anne pulled back and waved her off. "Sorry for the pity party everyone. Of all people, I should know better.

"Anyway..." Anne continued. "I spoke with Gerritson when I got back. He said Dad needs to keep the pills down for a long as he can. And to drink a lot of water. He also said Dad's going to slip back and forth more often until the pills take full effect, which is usually two to three weeks. After that, Dad should have fewer episodes, and those he does have will be for shorter durations."

Mrs. Tuttle gave a rare smile. "That sounds encouraging."

Anne gave a quick shake of her head. "Not really, Gerritson also warned me that the longer he's on the pills the more likely it would affect his heart and liver."

"Aww crap!" Eleanor said as she popped a Nicorette gum into her mouth and dropped the rest of the plastic strip into her bag.

Just then, Jim left his bedroom and with a concerned expression walked down the hall, out the door and into the back yard.

Chapter 21

When I first awoke, I was confused as I didn't remember going to bed. In fact, the last thing I remember was arguing with Turtledove over her ridiculous claim that she didn't have any children. Then I heard some rustling on the other side of my bed and scooched over to investigate. As I looked over the side, Bosco O'Bama the Third slid out from under it.

"So there you are! Why did you hide under the bed when your mother came in?"

"I didn't want her to see me like this, you know, all beat up." he replied as he rose and brushed the dust bunnies from his shirt and pants.

"Did you hear what she said?" I asked. "Did you hear her say she doesn't have a son?"

Bosco rolled his eyes and nodded. "Yeah, I did. She's still mad at me."

"Why would she be mad at you?" My concern for the boy's welfare was noticeable in my voice. His overall pallor and constitution seemed sickly and weak, which made Turtledove's terseness all the more confusing.

"She's mad at me for not kicking Luke's ass," he said as he took a seat at the end of the bed. "Mom's a tough cookie. Fearless and strong. Always said I must find a way to win every battle. When I told her I was afraid of Luke... she... she looked so... disappointed." He lowered his head and wiped his eyes. "Like she was disgusted with me. She just stared at me for a moment, then shook her head, and walked away."

I nodded. As much as I love Turtledove, she can be a real, cold, pain in the ass sometimes. I told Bosco he

155

needed some rest, so I pulled him up to the pillows, and placed a blanket over him.

After tucking him in, I heard a tap on the window. I turned and was momentarily startled. At first I thought it was a large gray snake, but with a second look, I realized it was Gladys the elephant's trunk.

When she tapped a second time I waved, indicating I'd be with her in a minute.

Stepping out the back door and down the stairs, I smiled to let Gladys know I was willing to put our earlier unpleasantness behind us. It was then I noticed that the monkeys, Rosencrantz and Guildenstern were with her.

Nevertheless, I remained cordial and welcoming as I approached.

Then I saw the suitcases.

"A little late in the day for a friendly visit," I said, "but it's still good to see you. What's with the luggage? Planning a trip?"

With a melancholy look, Gladys slowly nodded and approached. "We need to talk," she said. She was carrying a six pack of tall boys, which meant she was going to need a little liquid courage to spit out what she had come to say.

Using her trunk, she cracked open a Budweiser and took a sip. Sitting on the deck steps, she crossed her legs in a very ladylike manner. Despite our differences, she always had class.

"As you know," she began, then took another sip, "we members of the wild kingdom have a heightened sense of danger. We can tell when earthquakes and wildfires and Jehovah Witnesses are coming and take appropriate action to protect ourselves."

156

I pulled a tall boy free and cracked it open, as did the monkeys. We raised and toasted each other, then had a sip. "Please continue," I said.

"Well, the thing is, our heightened sense of peril and need for self-preservation tells us that the time has come for us to explore…"

Rosencrantz spun and brought his monocle to his eye. "Oh for heaven's sakes, behemoth, just speak your piece and have done with it!" Being a British peer, he would not tolerate any shillyshallying. '**Have at it and into the breach**' he'd always say. Sugar-coating was not his style.

Surprised, and caught slightly off guard, I eyed them, not liking the way this was going. "What danger?" I asked. "And what makes you so sure there is any?"

"We're all feeling it," the transvestite Guildenstern said. "Cissy was so upset she began doing that over the water dance dolphins do with their tails and accidently sank an oil tanker."

"And then there is the Land o' the Future," Gladys said grimly.

"What about it!?" I said a little more intensely than I intended.

Rosencrantz stood. "See here, I don't much care for your tone!"

"My apologies," I said, far more interested in what Gladys had to say than getting into an argument with some stuffed-shirt monkey. "What's the problem with Land o' the Future?"

"It's no longer there," Gladys replied, taking a long swig.

I wasn't sure I heard her correctly. "Gone? How can an entire exhibit, spanning several miles… disappear? I was just there the other day with my grandson."

157

Rosencrantz sat back down and said, "Be that as it may, my good man, it's gone. All of it. Nary a trace. It is as if it never existed."

Guildenstern then said, "We believe it disappeared because, well, there is no future. At least not here. So we've decided to find another place to live."

I was stunned. "What other place? Where will you go and how will you get there? Are the other animals in Land o' the Jungle leaving too?" I placed my beer on the step. My stomach was queasy, and the alcohol wasn't helping.

Gladys stood and said, "We're going to ride on Cissy's back through the Whateverland Canal then out into the Indian Ocean. We contacted Chief Wild Eagle of the Hekawis Tribe and he has assured us safe passage through Indian Territory. As for the other animals, most have already left. They just didn't have the heart to tell you. The few that remain will likely follow in a day or so."

She wrapped her trunk around my shoulder and gave me a gentle squeeze. "I'm sorry, but us wild animals aren't known for our sensitivity and manners. If you like, you're welcome to join us."

I patted her trunk and said, "Thank you, but if things get rough, me and my family will take the trip with Cap'n Spaulding and Polly.

Rosencrantz adjusted his monocle and eyed me suspiciously. "You are aware his ship is called The Charon?"

I thought for a moment then said. "No, I wasn't. But what does the name of his ship have to do with anything?"

"Most likely nothing," Rosencrantz replied with a smug expression I didn't care for. "Well, we've said what needed to be said, so we'll be on our way."

As they finished their beers and placed the empty cans on the deck stairs, I said, "Well, I won't try and stop you, but I think you're making a mistake. In any case, you're always welcome back should things not turn out as expected."

"That's very kind of you," Gladys said, as she picked up several suitcases with her trunk. "And we all hope you take what we said to heart. Danger IS coming. The predators are gathering and the die has been cast."

I nodded, and as they headed down the path, I overheard Rosencrantz say, "The die has been cast? What in blazes do you know about casting dice? You can't even make a fist."

I rolled my eyes. *I give that little party about twenty minutes before they start tearing into each other and stomp back to the Land o'the Jungle.*

Not knowing what to do with that bit of news and with Turtledove having left for work, I decided to check on Bosco O'Bama the Third. When I entered the bedroom I saw the pillow and blankets were on the floor and the window was open.

Then I saw *it*.

It was a note on a white sheet of paper laying in the center of the bed. Written in red crayon were the words:

I got the kid. If you ever want to see him again meet me at the beam of light and come alone.

LUKE

I looked outside. It had suddenly gotten dark.

159

Chapter 22

"Dad? Dad? Time to wake up. Mrs. Tuttle has breakfast ready, and I have an appointment with..." Anne was going to say *my lawyer*, but stopped, not wanting to concern her father with her legal problems.

Jim's eyes popped open, and he sat up with a confused look. "Huh?" He looked around. Then pushed back his hair and studied Anne as she stood over him.

"You okay?" she asked. "You seem a little confused. Do you know who I am?"

He shot her a dismissive sneer. "Of course I know who you are! I'm no..." He stopped, shook his head. "I'm sorry. I had an upsetting dream, that's all. And I don't remember going to bed."

Anne went over and opened the blinds to let the sun in. "Another bad dream huh? What was this one about?"

Jim momentarily squinted from the glare then pulled off the blankets, sat up and slid his feet into his slippers.

"It's starting to fade. But I do remember one thing. Some guy named Luke was threatening me, or someone I know, I'm... I'm not sure."

Although Jim hadn't noticed, Anne visibly paled when he mentioned Luke. That was one part of their lives no one in the family wanted to revisit. She changed the subject. "Well, take all the time you need to get ready, Breakfast can keep."

She smiled, patted her father on the shoulder, and made her way out of Jim's room. After closing the door behind her she placed her hand on the wall and let out a deep, mournful sigh.

As Anne reentered the kitchen, Elle asked, "Dad up?" She was in the middle of stabbing pancakes and dropping them on her plate. She was wearing her red bathrobe with her hair tied in a top knot.

Anne gave a half-hearted nod, then said, "He's going to need a minute." She took a seat at the table, but instead of diving into the selection of breakfast goodies Mrs. Tuttle had laid out, she turned and stared out the window.

As Mrs. Tuttle brought her a cup of coffee, Elle picked up on Anne's troubled expression.

"If you're worried about your meeting with Scott Tremaine, don't be," Elle said as she reached for the syrup and popped open the cap, "He's a great guy, and I'm sure he'll get this thing with that thankless bitch thrown out in no time."

"Huh?" Anne said turning.

"Your meeting with Tremaine," Elle said as she finished pouring the syrup and placed the bottle back. "You look worried."

Anne waved her hand. "No, no, it's not that. I've dealt with lawyers hundreds of times, it's what Dad just said that's got me a bit rattled."

With a concerned look Elle leaned in. "What did he say?"

Anne spooned a teaspoon of sugar into her coffee and stirred. "He said he had a dream that someone named Luke was threatening him." She emphasized the word Luke.

Elle grimaced. "Whoa! That's not good. You think it's related? You know to…"

"I know what you're referring to," Anne tersely replied. "To tell you the truth, I don't know what to think. Maybe it's just something out of nowhere. You know how jumbled his thoughts get. He said the dream was fading, so

161

maybe he'll forget about it by the time he comes out for breakfast."

Elle dunked her toast into her coffee and took a quick bite. "I certainly hope so."

Having overheard, Mrs. Tuttle wondered if she should ask about this Luke person, just in case Jim brought it up later, but after seeing both women's frightened concerns, she decided it was better to leave well enough alone.

They all looked up as Jim entered the kitchen. "Morning, my girls. Mrs. Tuttle. Ooo, that coffee smells good." As Mrs. Tuttle pulled a cup from the cupboard and made her way to the coffeemaker, Jim took a seat at the table and said, "I think the meds are helping. I'm starting to remember certain aspects of the places I go on my..." he smiled and patted Anne on the shoulder. "On what you call my excursions."

As Elle cut into her pancakes, she said, "That sounds encouraging," Afraid that he might ask about Luke, she quickly changed the subject. It wasn't something she wanted to talk about, but it needed to be discussed while Jim was thinking clearly. His take on the matter was vital to her decision.

"Dad, I have good news and bad news," she said as she wiped her lips, crumpled her napkin and placed it on the side of her plate.

He thanked Mrs. Tuttle as she placed the coffee in front of him then turned to Elle and gave her his full attention. "Go on."

"Goldenrod is in the process of purchasing the Great Experience Cruise Lines and if it goes through as planned, I will be installed as the company's chief operating officer." She drained her coffee. "It's one heck of an

162

opportunity, especially since I'm only thirty-one-years-old. Plus the salary bump is impressive."

Jim tapped his crooked index finger to his lips, "Sounds great but you said good news AND bad news," he said opening his napkin and placing it on his lap. "I'm very happy for you and know you'll do great, you always do." He tilted his head. "And the bad news is?"

She gave a half-hearted shrug. "The job is in Manhattan. If I take it, I'll have to move there."

This time Jim shrugged. As he ladled sugar into his coffee, he said, "I don't see where there's a problem." He stirred, then took a sip "You have always been a go-getter. Actually both of you are. I wasn't bothered when Anne moved to Albany to be closer to *her* work, so why should I be concerned if you do the same?"

He smiled and looked to see their response.

He noticed neither daughter nor Mrs. Tuttle was smiling back.

He put down the cup. "Oh, the elephant in the room," he said. "You're concerned about what might happen to me if you're no longer around to tag team with your sister and Mrs. Tuttle. Is that it?"

He smiled again, but when the smile still wasn't returned, he suspected the reason was because they didn't think he was taking the matter as seriously as he should.

He bowed his head. "I apologize. I'd forgotten how disruptive my medical condition can be." He looked up, "Regardless, Elle, if you want the job, take the job. You have to think of your future. I've already had my life, and it's been a great one. I was able to do everything I ever wanted. And yes, I am aware that some of the decisions your mother and I made didn't always turn out, but overall, we did pretty good. We were never homeless, without food, or without power or utilities."

"But you subjected us to a childhood of basic cable, you monster!" Anne said with a laugh. Her appetite had returned and she was adding sausages to the pancakes already on her plate.

"And restricted internet access!" Elle said with a feigned look of disapproval. "How were we suppose to see hot guys in the buff with restricted internet?" She gave a theatrical pout. "I don't know if I can ever forgive you for that."

Jim spun his hands the way television people do to wrap up. "Well, before you both cut me out of the will, just remember that you might have kids of your own someday, and then we'll see just how well you two do as parents."

Elle flicked her hand dismissively. "And give you the opportunity to say I told you so?" she shook her head, struck a regal pose and said in an affected British accent, "I think not!"

After they finished breakfast and Mrs. Tuttle began clearing the table, Jim said. "Look, I know I've been a problem. So while I have a clear head and am able to give one last morsel of fatherly advice, I say again, if you want that job, Eleanor, you take that job!"

"But Dad," Anne said, "we can't just…"

Jim waved her off. "No, Anne. We can't let emotions get in the way of sound judgment. My condition is terminal. Pretty soon I'll no longer recognize either of you or be able to tend to my personal hygiene. You're trying to bail out a ship that's going to sink no matter what you do. And once it does, what will you have accomplished? Elle will have passed on a lucrative position that would have secured her future and Anne, you would've had to shoulder unnecessary added pressure while trying to perform an already highly stressful and dangerous job."

Jim picked up his coffee and rose from the table. "So I want you both to promise me that you're going to start making preparations for hospice. Don't allow my condition to dissuade you from doing what has to be done. Promise?"

Elle's eyes teared up. "Dad, I don't know if…" Tears began running down her cheek.

Anne took Elle's hand. "We promise, Dad."

Jim looked at his youngest daughter as she dabbed her eyes with a tissue. "Honey?"

Elle sniffed and nodded, "Yes, Dad, I promise."

Good!" Jim said with a sharp nod. "Now, one last thing. Does the name Luke ring any bells with either of you? I know I don't always think clearly but for some reason I've got it in my head that someone named Luke is a danger to our family."

Anne said, "It was just a dream, Dad. You shouldn't worry about it. No one named Luke is trying to hurt us. And if there was, I'd remind him that I have a gun, a badge and a black belt in karate."

Elle sniffed and tried to smile. "There you go! Problem solved. So don't give it another thought."

Jim felt that made sense. "You're probably right. It's likely another side effect of the meds. Speaking of which…" Jim said as he grimaced, "… time for another batch." As always Mrs. Tuttle was two steps ahead of him. He saw his pills were laid out on the kitchen counter, accompanied by a glass of water and a small muffin.

165

Chapter 23

Two days after their initial meeting, Scott Tremaine called Anne and said they needed to talk right away. Following their original discussion, a new piece of evidence had been admitted. It was the unmarked car's dashboard video which had recorded the gun battle. It painted a different picture than Anne's recollections of her confrontation with the gunmen.

Tremaine's Albany, New York, office was only a few blocks east of the governor's mansion and in one of the lofty skyscrapers constructed in the 1970's during Governor Nelson Rockefeller's administration. When Anne arrived at Tremaine, Lauder and Wells, the receptionist escorted her to Scott Tremaine's office. Once inside, he greeted her, and directed her to the seat in front of his desk, then returned to his chair.

Normally Anne would have taken note of how handsome and professional looking her attorney was. With just a touch of gray at the temples of his jet black hair and eyes almost as blue as her sister's, he was, as Elle described, quite the hunk, However, romance was the last thing on her mind, and she appreciated the fact that once seated, Scott got right to business.

He explained that although the shooting followed police procedure and was completely justified, the dashcam video itself did not portray her well. "In fact," he added, "it's quite damning."

"In what respect?" she asked as she placed her pocketbook on the floor and opened her coat. Her face suddenly filled with concern.

"Well," Tremaine said, pulling at his cuffs, "let's watch the video so you can see for yourself." Although

166

smiling and cordial, the forty-two year old lawyer couldn't completely mask his irritation. He felt Anne had not been upfront regarding the *entire* story.

Over the first few minutes of the video, Anne felt quite proud. It clearly showed the gunman ramming her car and firing several bullets at her, yet she remained calm and professional. She had pressed the emergency response button on the car's dash, which alerted the area police that an officer was in danger, then deactivated the manual control of the dashboard camera and activated the 'Follow me' signal that had the camera lock onto the signal from her gun holster. It recorded her every move.

She opened the driver's-side door, slid to the ground, and fired several rounds from under the car into the mini-van's tires.

As the mini-van slid sideways down the hill, Anne crawled to the front driver's side panel and popped up to assess the situation. That's when the camera resumed recording her.

Since the camera was set to follow *her*, it did not show what the gunmen were doing, and because the windows were closed on Anne's car, the gunman's threats to kill the daughter were mostly inaudible, as were the other daughter's plea to the gunman not to kill her sister.

What it did show was a very stern-faced Anne taking careful aim and firing one bullet. Then the camera showed her approaching the minivan and firing non-stop. At one point, she picked up the dead gunman's pistol and emptied it into the driver along with her own.

"You fired seventeen rounds into the minivan," Tremaine said coldly as he stopped the video player. "According the video, the man was obviously dead when your fourth round took off the top of his head. So I have to ask, why did you feel such excessive force was necessary? Frankly, this video portrays you, not as a police officer doing her duty but an executioner carrying out a vendetta."

Anne took a moment to collect her thoughts. Her stomach had become a ball of electricity. She, too, was startled at the ferocity of her attack on the driver's-side gunman. She brought a shaking hand to her mouth, took a deep breath and said, "This video only tells half the story. It doesn't show the gunman pressing his gun against a six-year-old girl's head and threatening, very loudly and determinedly, that unless I dropped my gun he was going to blow that little girl's head off. It doesn't show the child's father lying at the bottom of the hill with the better part of his skull shot off."

Anne took another breath. "The camera also doesn't show me being hit in the chest by two of the driver's rounds."

"Yes, but at no point did you give the driver the opportunity to surrender," Tremaine said with a suspicious look. When she glared at him he said, "I'm sorry, but these are the questions the jury is going to want answered, should this go to trial."

Anne drew a breath. "It was the driver who opened fire at me when I blocked the mini-van's attempted escape. He had no idea my car's windows were reinforced, or that my doors and sidepanels were as well. He was trying very hard to kill me. Do you understand?" She paused for a moment, then continued. "Do you understand that he made every possible effort to take my life!?" Her voice rose in anger. "And now you're saying that because he didn't succeed, I should have risked my life to give him the opportunity to surrender?"

"I understand your position, detective," Tremaine said, extending his hands in a compassionate gesture. He rose, walked around his desk and sat on its edge. "However, you're being sued in civil court for using excessive force and for endangering the lives of Mrs. Blanchart and her two daughters."

Anne bristled. "I *saved* the lives of Mrs. Blanchet and her two daughters, and now this greedy bitch is suing the department for millions and ruining my career in the process. So let's cut to the chase: are you telling me you can't win this case or that you'd like to drop me as your client?"

"Neither," he replied as he leaned forward and eyed Anne directly. "I can win this case, and if I have to call the two kids and Mrs. Blanchet herself to the stand, I'll do it in a heartbeat. But regardless of the verdict, your career as a detective is likely over. Even if Mrs. Blanchet's suit is thrown out, that video has destroyed any possibility of advancement, because if you are ever forced to draw your gun again and take someone's life, that video will circulate like wildfire. It paints you as a rogue cop, maybe even a vigilante. So the reality question is, 'Are you okay with being a desk jockey until retirement?'"

As Scott waited for her answer, Anne felt the ball of electricity die down, and her anxiety dissipate.

Tremaine started to say, "The reason for this is strictly political, The Albany…" but Anne cut him off.

"I don't need to know the reason," she said. "It is what it is. So," she added as she rose to her feet, "here's why I kept firing. I knew I had been hit, not once but twice. I had no way of knowing if the bullets pierced my vest or not, so I had to make sure the driver was dead because if I succumbed and it turned out he was wearing a vest and his

169

held, he would very likely use the family as hostages just as his partner had. And maybe this gunman WOULD have blown that little girl's head off." She took a breath. "I couldn't take that chance. So I did what I had to do. That's all there is to it. Is there anything else we need to discuss?"

Surprised at her calm description of the event, Tremaine stood and said, "Nothing that can't wait. I should point out that you can petition the department to review the case if you feel you are being treated unfairly or are being prevented from advancing. The legal procedure..."

"No need," she said, buttoning her coat and grabbing her pocketbook. "Regardless of the outcome, I'm done being a police officer. Because of what happened with the Blanchet family, I will never again risk my life or well-being for a stranger. I've had it with all those smug sonsabitches. They're nothing more than a bunch of candy-assed intellectual scumbags who have never had to risk their life for a fellow human being, yet somehow believe they have the right to question the decisions an officer makes while under fire. Fuck'em!" She swung her pocketbook strap over her shoulder. "You said you can win the case. Good. You do that. As for me, once the matter is settled, I'll apply for early retirement and start reviewing other employment options.

She turned and walked out of Tremaine's office without another word.

170

Chapter 24

The following day, Eleanor was inside the corporate jet winging its way from Albany to New York City. It was a quick trip, usually no more than thirty minutes, and was rapidly becoming a regular thing because Goldenrod's headquarters were in Albany and Great Experiences' were in Manhattan.

She sat at the round table in the jet's center reviewing some papers with Scott Tremaine, CEO Elliot Chase and two accountants she had just been introduced to. In mid-business conversation, Elliot suddenly asked Eleanor how her father was doing.

She took a moment before answering. Not that she didn't have a ready answer, but she was concerned Elliot would say something insensitive, which he often did. Eleanor, in turn, would be sorely tempted to call him an mean-spirited douche-bag, which he often was.

His beak like nose, beady eyes and blubbery lips reminded her of one of those sea creature that live in the deepest areas of the ocean. Nevertheless, he was the boss so it was in her best interest to give a short and cordial response.

"We're considering having him admitted to hospice," she replied, not looking up from the paperwork, and hoping to kill the conversation as quickly as possible. She turned to Tremaine. "When do Rhinehoff and the rest of Great Ex's legal department meet with you and our people?"

Eleanor didn't really need that information, but wanted to get the topic of her father off the table.

It didn't work.

171

Before Scott could answer, Elliot said, "I think putting your father in hospice as quickly as possible would be to everyone's advantage," he said as casually as if discussing where to store winter clothing. "Your absence last week put a great burden on us all, and your ins and outs because of your sister's injuries only added to the problem. If I were you, I would make every effort to ensure it doesn't happen again."

Eleanor simply nodded and pretended to be preoccupied with the paperwork. Inside, however, she was seething. *You ugly, arrogant prick! I know the game you're playing. This is revenge for that dust-up we had over the phone last week when I reminded you that you had plenty of time to prepare for my absence and that your problems were of your own making. Which they were.* She wondered, *Why is it always little, bitter, rat-faced turds like Elliot who wind up being the person in charge?*

"Did you hear me, Eleanor?" Elliot said. His beady eyes squinted and his blubbery lips thinned. He wanted to make sure everyone on the plane knew who was the boss, particularly Eleanor.

She stopped and looked up, wearing her most practiced pokerface. Without the slightest indication that she wanted to tear him a new asshole and forcibly jam his head into it, she said, "Yes, Elliot, I heard every word. You made your point clearly and cleanly." She went back to her paperwork.

"Good!" he said smugly. "I certainly wouldn't want there to be any misunderstandings." He bent over a bit to make sure to catch her eye.

Eleanor looked up again. "Nope, no misunderstanding." Maintaining her pokerface she held her gaze, knowing that anything Elliot added at this point

172

would make him look petty and vindictive, which he was. But he didn't want a plane filled with lawyers and accountants to know that.

Seeing that Elliot realized he had played that hand as far as it could go, she resumed her conversation with Scott.

She knew, however, that this wasn't over.

Eleanor entered one of the conference rooms at Great Experiences offices and found herself alone with Scott Tremaine. They were the first to arrive for yet another meeting.

"So," Eleanor said casually as she settled in and draped her arm over the back of her chair, "how's my sister's case shaping up? She gets nasty if she goes without working for too long."

Her attitude was light and breezy, but that quickly changed when Scott, who was standing at the counter pouring himself a cup of coffee replied, "I can't discuss your sister's case. I'm sure you know that, but I don't think your sister is as anxious to get back to work as you think."

Eleanor's eyes widened and she dropped her arm into her lap. "Really? She's actually considering leaving the police force?"

Scott shrugged, walked to the table and sat down across from her. "Like I said, you'd have to ask your sister." He shook a sugar packet, tore it open, poured it into his coffee and stirred. "This experience has been a life-changer for Anne. What I saw yesterday was an angry and bitter woman, who, I should add, has every right to be."

*

173

Jim sat at the kitchen table with Mrs. Tuttle. She had made tea and he was having a cup with her, even though he didn't like tea all that much.

After adding milk and sugar he said, "I'm sorry for all the grief I've caused you over the last... what's it been? Eleven, twelve months? I watched the videos and... well... He stopped as his face turned red from embarrassment.

"No need to apologize," Mrs. Tuttle said, wiping her hands on a napkin and then each figure individually. "I'm a caregiver. It's my job to see to the needs of people like yourself. Usually I tend to Alzheimer or dementia patients, but because your condition is unique, I've had to acquire an entirely new set of skills. Yes, it's been challenging at times, but also rewarding. I see a lot of joy in your face when you go to your special place. And I also see a lot of love for that child you seem to have with you. And I've gotten to know you and your lovely daughters, which is a memory I'll always cherish."

She finished her tea, rose from the table and collected the dishes and silverware. "Would you like to go for a ride?"

Jim didn't know how to answer. "Is that allowed? I mean, considering my condition?"

She nodded as she flipped up the top of the silver garbage can and tossed in the two used tea bags. "We go out semi-regularly. Usually it's for doctors' appointments and medical tests, but we sometimes go for rides, if for no other reason than a change of scenery."

He considered it although not quite sure it was a good idea.

Mrs. Tuttle smiled. "You're thinking about those videos again?" She shook her head. "You needn't worry.

174

My vehicle is a handicap van. When we go out, you're secured into your seat, so should you happen to have an episode, you won't be able to move around. And if that happens, I'll cut the ride short and we'll come home."

Before he could reply, she said, "Oh, I just remembered, you got mail." She looked around. "Now where did I put... oh, that's right." She reached up, removed an envelope from the top of the refrigerator and brought it over.

Jim took it from her, examined it, and said, "Probably just a bill." The return address in the corner had no name, just a P.O. Box number and the city and state.

"Hmmm," he said, now curious. "I wonder who..." His voice trailed off as he ripped open the sealed flap and eyed it's contents. "Looks like a sales come-on," he said as he pulled out the papers. On the front page was a large banner that read **Super Year-End Close-Out Sale.**

"Yeah, just as I thought" he said, perusing the papers. "They want me to trade in my Mustang for a brand new..."

His voice trailed off.

Wait a minute, he said to himself. *That isn't what it says.* His eyes widened. He read it again.

I got the kid. If you ever want to see him again meet me at the beam of light and come alone.

LUKE

It was written in red crayon.

No... No it wasn't, he suddenly realized. When he held the paper vertically the red printing ran down the page. It wasn't crayon. It was... blood.

Mrs. Tuttle saw the color drain from Jim's face. "Are you all right?" She approached and took the letter from his

175

hands and gave it a quick read. All three pages. He was right. It was a sales come-on. The letter was touting Glenstown Motors year end sale and all the benefits of trading in his present Mustang and driving home in a BRAND NEW CAR!

She dropped it on the table but he picked it up and read it again with trembling hands.

Mrs. Tuttle sat next to him. "Jim, I want you to read the letter out loud."

He looked up, turned the first page of the letter to her, and pointed.

She shook her head. "I'm not wearing my glasses. You'll have to read it to me." The fact was, Mrs. Tuttle didn't wear glasses, but she was pretty sure Jim was in no condition to remember that.

He quickly inhaled and nodded. "It says: I got the kid, if you ever want to see him again meet me at the beam of light and come alone. It's signed, Luke."

Mrs. Tuttle nodded. "Do you know who Luke is?"

Jim dropped the letter on the table and pressed his hands to his temple. "No, I don't! But I think I'm supposed to." His face twisted with worry and concern.

Mrs. Tuttle reached over and placed a gentle hand on Jim's arm. "Take a deep cleansing breath. We'll figure this out. Who Luke is will probably come to you, but first, who is the kid Luke took?"

With tear-filled eyes, Jim took cupped Mrs. Tuttle's hand and said, "I'm so sorry. I only left him alone for a minute. I was outside talking with Gladys. It never occurred to me that this Luke person was crazy enough to sneak in through the window and kidnap him."

Mrs. Tuttle leaned in, anxious to get answers before Jim became incomprehensible. Who?" she asked. "Who did Luke kidnap?"

Jim let go of her hands and bowed his head. "He's got your boy, Turtledove. He's got your son, Bosco O'Bama the Third!"

Jim heard the phone ring. He turned and charged from his seat.

Mrs. Tuttle bolted from the table. "What's the matter?"

He reached for the phone. "It could be the kidnapper. Maybe he wants me to bring money. If so, I'm going to have to drive to the bank!"

Mrs. Tuttle nodded and went to the sink as Jim picked up the phone. "Hello? Hello?" he said nearly shouting.

There was a pause then a weak voice said, "Gam'pa, please help me!"

Jim momentarily covered the receiver and turned to Mrs. Tuttle. "It's Bosco!" he said.

Mrs. Tuttle nodded and brought over a small glass of water. "Drink this," she said. "You don't want your voice drying out while talking with the kidnapper."

That made perfect sense, so Jim took the glass and quickly downed its contents. He kept the phone pressed to his ear. "I'm coming to get you, son. Just tell me where you are. Tell me, and I'll come get you."

"You know where I am," the boy said in a whisper, then coughed. "I am where I always am. I'm in in the part of Whateverland where the bug stung you. Remember?"

"Yes! Yes!" Jim quickly answered. "I remember! In the Rest Area!"

"Hurry, Gam'pa," the boy said with a trembling voice. "I'm hurt pretty bad."

177

Jim face reddened with rage. "I'm coming, Bosco, and when I get there, I'm going to kill that sonavabitch with my bare hands! Hang in there, son. I'm on my way!"

Chapter 25

The place was surprisingly clean, orderly and very modern. Anne expected some run down hell-hole, a shitty last-stop dumpsite where those who could no longer play the Game of Life were scooped up and drop-kicked into the hands of their Creator.

This place seems all right, Anne thought as she surveyed her surroundings. Steel and glass, polished marble; all very, very professional. *And likely very, very expensive too.*

Just then a light-skinned African-American woman noticed her. She turned, approached with a pleasant smile and said, "Hello, I'm Jennifer Gavin, Patient Services. May I help you?"

Anne pulled her badge from her coat, showed it to the woman and said "I'm Detective Anne August of the Albany Police Department. I called earlier about possibly placing my father in your facility." Anne made sure the woman had a good look at the badge. A gold shield often garnered better service and less bullshit.

The woman paled at the sight of the badge but quickly regained her composure now that the conversation appeared to be about a potential patient.

"You probably spoke with our patient-liaison, Amanda Paris," the woman said, her ready smile returning. "Come this way and I'll take you to her."

As they walked through the hallways, Anne looked into the rooms and saw they were all as clean and orderly as the lobby, but the expressions of the loved ones visiting their dying relatives and friends were anything **but** clean and orderly. They were a messy hodge-podge mixture of

179

horror, sadness, fear, desperation and panic—all covered by a thin mask of pleasant smiles and kindly concern.

Something raked against the inside of her stomach and a faint taste of bile gurgled at the back of her throat. She took a breath as Jennifer prattled on about NorthCountry Care's many attributes as if it were a luxury resort or 5 star hotel instead of a death house.

More like a roach motel Anne thought. *People check in, but they don't check out.*

She thought of her late brother, Bob, and how he had joked about their father's request to place a pillow over his face and pump two bullets into his head should he ever be stricken by a long, lingering illness.

Seems a great deal more merciful than what goes on here.

Suddenly the orderliness and cleanliness annoyed her. Everything appeared so pleasant when, in reality, it was a house of horrors. People were dying horrible deaths here. In some of the rooms, she saw skeletons that were once people writhing in pain even though they were drugged to the point of being damn near comatose.

And some were children.

My God… children.

Please don't kill my sister! the little girl had shouted.

Anne's stomach quickly resembled one of those balls in the old horror movies that had tentacles of electricity dancing around their surfaces.

I'm not in any condition to be handling this. I'm not emotionally ready. Eleanor should be here or Mrs. Tuttle. But, she remembered, *Eleanor is dead center in the biggest deal of her career and Mrs. Tuttle isn't a family member.*

Shit!

180

It was then the pleasant-faced woman directed her to the inside of a cozy (yet still very orderly) looking office and announced that Ms. Paris would be with her directly.

Less than a minute later, Amanda Paris appeared wearing the same smile Jennifer had, and that annoyed Anne even more. *How can you smile when everyone around you is dying a slow, agonizing death?* she thought. *How can you work here? How could any human being with feelings and emotions work here?*

But when Ms. Paris introduced herself, Anne pulled it together, returned the smile, and cordially shook the woman's outstretched hand. The handshake annoyed her, too. It was too clinical, too methodical. It was like pressing the flesh with a robot.

Pump the brakes, Annie girl. This isn't about you—it's about Dad.

Once both women were seated, Amanda Paris, with her slightly greyish auburn hair pulled back into a bun said through lips that Anne thought were a little too red, "Welcome to NorthCountry Care, Ms. August, I brought some literature that explains our services and how they may benefit your father." She spread them on the desk for Anne to examine.

Anne scanned them, choose one, and began to read.

Still smiling, Ms. Paris said, "Over the phone, you explained that your father contracted a virus resulting in the swelling and deterioration of brain tissue. That's quite rare. I mention this because that rarity means we have no way of estimating how long your father will be needing our services."

Anne looked up. "So what are you saying?" Her words came out a little too brusk, and she hoped Ms. Paris hadn't noticed.

The woman's smile faded and an all-business expression took its place. This was a relief to Anne who simply couldn't stomach the affected sugary pleasantness much longer.

"Allow me to apologize in advance if my answer seems insensitive, but to be clear, all our patients die. People are brought here because there is nothing more medical science can do for them. Our job is to ease their pain, if possible, and present them with a comfortable environment where they can pass away in peace. Because your father's condition is so rare, we have no way of knowing how long he'll be with us. An extended stay can become quite costly." She opened a manila file folder, took her reading glasses from the chain around her neck, placed them on her nose and gave a quick read of its contents. "From what I can see, your father's insurance is adequate, hospice care however, is only covered for ninety days. After that, it's out-of-pocket. It also says that you and your sister, Eleanor, are guaranteeing payment should our services be required beyond the ninety day period. Is that correct?" she asked, returning her glasses to her chest.

Anne nodded, but those talons were raking the inside of her stomach again. She had no intention of returning to duty once her ribs healed and this bullshit with the Blanchet family was resolved. She had about thirty grand in savings and a pretty healthy 401K if she had to tap into that, plus Eleanor would soon be making more money than God, so things should be okay, but... *But what if Dad lives six more months, or even a year? I'd be wiped out, unemployed, my future income garnished, and he'd still need care! Even with all the money Eleanor will be making, she's going to need a healthy chunk of that just to live in New York City.*

182

"Here are the papers we'll need signed and authorized by your father's primary care physician," Ms. Paris said, handing the file folder across her desk. As Anne reviewed it, the patient-liaison sat back and steepled her fingers. "By all means have them reviewed by your attorney, and have him explain our insurance coverage. You should note that because this is a hospice, we have very little. This is because people die here. Regularly. And often not from the disease itself. Sometime they get up in the middle of the night disoriented, fall and break a bone or two. Sometimes it's the painkillers. We try to make them a comfortable as possible, but there is only so much a body greatly ravaged by disease can endure. Sometimes they take their own lives. We have learned that if a person is determined to commit suicide, there is little you can do to stop them. They always find a way."

Anne simply nodded. She couldn't argue the point. Especially since that's how her grandfather hit the exit ramp.

Anne stood and placed the folder in her pocketbook. "Thank you, Ms. Paris," she said shaking the woman's hand. "You've been most helpful."

With her stomach feeling like it was manufacturing rivulets of hot lava, sure to be looking for an exit very soon, Anne was quickly on her way.

Chapter 26

The day's negotiations between Goldenrod and Great Experiences Cruise Lines ended early that afternoon due to some accounting matter that needed to be resolved before the acquisition could continue. So with time to kill, Eleanor left the Great X building and started along the busy streets of Manhattan with the intention of getting to know the Big Apple—her soon-to-be new home—a little better.

She marveled at the massive skyscrapers and took in the sights and sounds for a little over twenty minutes, then realized the city's ultrafast pace and cacophony of flashing billboards and sharp noises were going to take some getting used to. Not looking to be overwhelmed, she decided she had had enough and planned to head home. Just as she was about to hail a cab, her cell phone rang. She pulled it from her pocket, checked the number, and not recognizing it, considered letting it go to voice mail.

But the fact that the call was from a 212 area code intrigued her. She didn't know anyone in Manhattan, so who would be calling? *Probably a wrong number*, she thought. As she stopped to consider her next move, she was bumped from behind, and as the man walked past, he threw up his hands and said, "What the hell did ya stop for, lady?"

Startled, she watched as he pushed past several other pedestrians and into the busy street where a cab blared it's horn at him. He slammed his hands on the cab's hood and bellowed, "I'm in the crosswalk. What the hell's your problem?" Then broke into a trot to the other side.

As the crowds quickly stepped around her she ducked into a building's entranceway to avoid getting jostled again and to cut down on the noise and other distracting clatter.

She looked down and saw her phone's voicemail icon was lit.

Now she *was* curious. *It's got to be a wrong number,* she told herself.

But what if one of Tremaine's New York lawyer buddies asked for my number? I could be missing out on a great opportunity. Some fun, some drinks, and who knows?

She leaned against the brick façade while mulling her options, then said, "Ahh... what the hell" and pressed the V-mail icon.

'You have ONE new message,' the electronic voice said. Eleanor smirked as it ran though the options nobody ever needs and whose sole purpose is to eat up minutes.

When the voice mail did connect, Eleanor was startled by its content.

*Hello, Ms. August. This is Jane Haouk of Executive Hunters. You may have heard of us. We're the headhunting firm with the tagline, **We Always Bag the Big Ones**. I read in The Wall Street Journal that you're being promoted to the Chief Operating Officer for Goldenrods latest acquisition, Great Experiences Cruise Lines. Congratulations! However, before you accept the position, I'd like to talk to you about an another opportunity that you'd not only be perfect for, but will also put you in line for the top spot when their present CEO retires in three years. I assume you'll be visiting Manhattan in the near future, and I would appreciate it if you would call me when you do. My number is...*

185

Eleanor ended the call. Her phone automatically stored all her caller's numbers, so making note of the number wasn't necessary.

Years ago, Eleanor would have ignored the message and erased the number due to her loyalty to her employer. But that was before Elliot Chase became CEO. She was sure she could have handled the top job but hadn't been considered because of her age. But she was in her thirties now and clearly a threat to Elliot's position.

He knew it and she knew it, and Elliot took threats seriously. Ergo his summoning her to the office when he knew she wouldn't be able to come and the snide remarks on the corporate jet.

She also knew why Elliot greenlighted her promotion. It would get her out of Goldenrod's headquarters, giving him the opportunity to badmouth her plans for Great Ex to the board.

Still leaning against the wall, she brought her hand to her chin and considered the possibility that Elliot had one of Great Ex's administrative assistants make the call just to see if Eleanor would take the bait.

Mulling her options, she again made her way down the busy streets of Times Square knowing full well that was certainly something Elliot would do.

Still...

She pressed the Google maps icon and said into the phone, "Executive Hunters, Manhattan." In less than a second, an address appeared and directions to the Executive Hunters offices from where she was standing.

"Whoa!" she said aloud when she realized she had her phone's GPS locator on and that Elliot could follow her every move. She disabled that feature, shut off her phone, reconsidered her plans to head home, and decided instead it was a nice day for a walk.

*

Anne sat on the deck bench, looking over the yard. In her hand was a cup of hot chocolate with a shot of Bourbon in it. Maybe two; she hadn't measured. She had a difficult decision to make and was still trying to convince herself that she actually had a choice. But the truth was, she didn't.

The events of last night made that choice for her.

She was in a melancholy mood when she arrived at her father's house late yesterday evening, having spent the better part of the day researching NorthCountry Care, reading the pamphlets and getting the required signature from Dr. Gerritson.

Upon returning, she found the house empty and her father's bedroom door locked.

Concerned, she quickly scooted from room to room and just as she was about to panic, saw Mrs. Tuttle sitting on the deck step, leaning against the deck railing.

Anne opened the back door and quickly stepped out. "Mrs. Tuttle, what's going on? Why is my father locked in his room?"

The matronly woman sighed, and slowly rose to her feet. She wiped her hands on her apron and pressed her back against the railing. "Your father and I were having such a nice day," she said with a somewhat sad expression. "One of his better days to tell the truth. Even talked about going for a ride. Then… geez." She shook her head.

Anne walked over and leaned against the railing beside her. "I assume he had one of his episodes?"

187

Mrs. Tuttle sighed again and nodded. "Only this one… well, it was especially difficult."

Concerned, Anne asked, "What happened? Is he all right?"

"Oh, *he's* fine. But I've got a wrenched back and several pulled muscles." She grimaced and leaned forward to rub the affected area.

As Anne began to offer her sympathy, the caregiver waved her off and sat back down on the steps. "I'm sorry but I've got to get off my feet." She took a breath and let it out. "The thing is, it was going so well. That is until I stupidly handed him that junk mail letter. Damn!" she spat. She then told her of his terrified reaction to what he *thought* it said. When she mentioned Luke's name, Anne paled and a troubled expression spread across her face.

"And if that's not bad enough," Mrs. Tuttle continued, pressing her hand against the small of her back, "he jumped up and grabbed the wall phone even though it hadn't rung. He thought it was Bosco on the line."

Again the caregiver paused for a moment and shook her head before reluctantly pressing-on. "I realized he was having a full-blown episode when he began talking about driving to the bank. And that he's wound up enough to force his way past me and maybe out into the street. So I squirt a good amount of the liquid sedative into a glass of water, hand it to him and he drinks it.

"I'm figuring that within two, three minutes he'll be out cold." She shook her head. "I gave him enough to drop a rhinoceros," she said trying to show how hard she tried to avert a calamity. "It didn't even slow him down. Then he said we have to rescue Bosco, and we'll need the Whateverland horses."

"Whateverland horses?" Anne asked, thoroughly confused. "What in blazes is that?".

Mrs. Tuttle momentarily looked away and tried to form a reply, but couldn't. "I'll explain in a bit. At least I will TRY to. Anyway, he said we have to go through the Whateverland Midway until we reach the Rest Area. Then, from there, past something that has to do with Harry Potter." She raises her hand, anticipating Anne's question. "Don't ask. I haven't a clue. Anyway, I'm figuring that as long as I stay alongside him, he won't go off the reservation, so to speak. So I play along and do as he says and wait for the damn sedative to kick in.

"Then he's on again about getting our horses from the Whateverland stables. And I say okay, BUT, we need to take a wheelchair with us. The real reason is because when the drugs *do* kick in, he's going to drop pretty quick, and when he does, I wanted that wheelchair under him. So he looks at me kind of queer, obviously questioning my motives, then suddenly says, "Oh that's right, Turtledove, Bosco may need medical attention. Good call!"

Mrs. Tuttle rolled her eyes. "So, I go back in the house, get the wheelchair from the closet, and charge out the back door hoping I won't find him on the ground.

"Was he?" Anne asked, taking a seat alongside her on the step.

Mrs. Tuttle shook her head. "Nope. My luck was holding. But he was slowly skipping around the back yard so I assume he thought he was on one of the horses, holding his hand out like he was holding my horse's rein."

She shruged. "Soooo, figuring the sedative HAS to take effect any minute now, I mount up and together we go skipping along on our faithful steeds side by side. Several more minutes pass..."

189

A look of deep concern appeared on Mrs. Tuttle's face and she momentarily stared off. "It was then I realize that the drug *has* taken effect, but the poor dear is fighting it with everything he can muster. His legs are getting wobbly and he's reeling a bit. So I say 'Jim, let's take a minute to rest. Let the horses catch their breath.'"

The caregiver's eyes suddenly become tear-filled. "He reaches over and takes my hand, looks at me and says. 'I don't know how much time I have left, but I will not die until I save your son. From the day you were born, I swore to Almighty God that I would always love and protect you. I will never let any harm come to you or my family, and your son is my family. If that means trading my life for his, then that's what will happen. And I don't care if you're a cop or a special agent or whatever. A father's first job is to protect his children, and I won't fail a second time."

She wipes the tears from her eyes. "He staggers forward, fighting the sedative, determined as all hell, but I can see he's about to go down, and I get the chair under him just in time. I yanked him and the chair up the three steps and rolled him into his bedroom and into his bed. I locked the door because I was exhausted and couldn't endure another round if he made a beeline for the street."

Anne took the caregiver's hand. "That was very, very kind of you. I don't know how to thank you."

Mrs. Tuttle gave Anne's hands a gentle squeeze and let them go. "You understand he thinks I'm you. At least to some extent."

Anne slowly nods. "That seem to be the case." She tilts her head to the house. "How much longer do you think he'll be out?"

190

"Oh, he's got a while yet. Hopefully he'll sleep through the night."

Anne opened her pocketbook and pulled out one of the pamphlets Ms. Paris gave her. "I stopped by NorthCountry Care today." She showed the broacher to Mrs. Tuttle, who gave it a quick perusal. "It seems like a good, well-run place. Elle and I will probably put Dad there when the time comes."

Mrs. Tuttle suddenly stared at her, wide-eyed.

"What?" Anne asked. "Is there something wrong with that place? What have you heard?"

Mrs. Tuttle quickly shook her head. "No, in fact I've heard many GOOD things about NorthCountry Care. My reaction…" she paused and bit her lower lip. "… was due to relief. You see, as of today, I'm giving you my two-weeks notice."

That was twenty-four hours ago.

Anne put the cup beside her, then placed her elbow on the arm of the bench and her hand under her chin. She had been up for most of the night checking on her father, making sure he was still breathing. Apparently, Mrs. Tuttle had dosed him pretty good because he was still groggy and lethargic a day later. By midafternoon, he was sitting in a chair in his bedroom, staring vacantly out the window.

She heard a car door slam and shortly afterward, the front door open and close.

Probably Eleanor, she thought.

It was. A minute or so later, Elle stepped out onto the back deck wearing her father's big blue and white cable-knit sweater. She had taken a liking to it since the first time she wore it and as Anne learned over the years, if Elle

191

liked a certain article of clothing, the best you could do was wave bye-bye before it became a permanent part of her younger sibling's wardrobe.

She signaled Anne to grab her hot-chocolate and scooch over. Once done she plopped down and exhaled. "Mrs. Tuttle left to get Dad's prescription refilled," she said crossing her outstreached legs and leaning back. "Said she had to use a lot of it yesterday to stop one of his freak-outs. Said you'd fill in the details. So what's the story, morning glory?"

"Doesn't matter," Anne replied with a far-off stare. "It's time for Dad to go to hospice."

Elle's eyes widened as she leaned in toward her sister. "Oh, man, what did he do? He didn't hit Mrs. Tuttle, did he?"

Anne shook her head, raised her cup of hot chocolate and took a sip. "No, nothing that spectacular. It's just that neither of us nor Mrs. Tuttle, is properly trained or equipped to handle him anymore."

Elle shrugged. "I don't know. I've always thought Mrs. Tuttle was pretty damn good at keeping Dad's coo-coo for Cocoa Puffs behavior under control. I mean, yeah she can be a little rough, but she…

Anne cut her off. "Mrs. Tuttle gave her notice yesterday."

Elle's jaw dropped. "Really!? Did she say why?

"She feels Dad has gotten to the point where he's too much for her to handle. The job's just too stressful."

Elle thought for a second and said, "Maybe if we offered her more money, we could…

Anne waved off the comment. "No, no. Dad was right. We've been trying to bail out a boat that's obviously going under. One way or another, this has to stop."

192

Elle eyed her sister suspiciously. "Okay, what happened? Why the change of heart?"

Anne turned, drew a breath, and began tapped her index finger against the cup. "Have you seen Dad? He still groggy from that enormous dose of sedative Tuttle gave him yesterday. I don't blame her, considering how bad things could have become, but that's proof, that, as well-meaning as our actions are, we'll just as likely kill Dad as save him. Look at it this way," Anne continued. "I have no idea if Dad's lethargy is from too much sedative or a worsening of his condition." She paused, took another sip, then said. "I checked out NorthCountry Care yesterday. Spoke with the patient liaison, a Ms. Paris."

As Elle processed this information, she pressed her lips together, then said, "Okay. So what did she tell you?"

Anne scratched the back of her neck, then pulled some of her hair off her blouse collar. "Mostly it was a sales pitch about how well they care for their patients. And the place really is immaculate and very well run. But the one thing that really struck me was the woman's plain talk about what hospice does. They are a place where people go to die. That's it, and it's accepted. Doesn't matter if they die from an accidental overdose, or breaking their necks falling out of bed, or hanging themselves in the janitor's closet like dear old Gramps. The people there are terminally ill. And when they die, the staff simply changes the sheets and rolls in the next one."

Elle pressed her hand to her chest. "Seems awful cold and uncaring."

Anne shrugged. "Maybe, but at hospice, dying is perfectly normal and they know how to prepare the patients and their loved ones for it. The thing is, if Mrs. Tuttle accidentally overdosed Dad yesterday, she could have been arrested. What if he punched that MRI tech? He'd be in jail instead of being properly cared for in hospice. Or what if he pushed past Mrs. Tuttle yesterday and ran out the front door, into the street and got hit by a car? More unnecessary misery for all involved." Anne bowed her head. "I love Dad, you love Dad, and even Mrs. Tuttle loves Dad and, a lot more than I thought. But keeping him here is selfish. Since he is going to die, better it be in a place where they know how to handle it than here or out in the street."

Anne expected Elle to make a case for some alternative. Instead, she became pensive and solemn. She took the cup from her sister's hand and before Anne could protest, swallowed a mouthful.

Her eyes bulged and her faced reddened as she handed the cup to her sister and began fanning air into her mouth. "Holy crap, Injun Joe, what's with the fire water?"

Anne merely shrugged, finished what remained, and placed the cup on the floor under the bench.

Several moments later, Elle, with a contemplative expression said, "You know, it's easy to talk about it and say it's for the best, which…" She held up her index finger to make her point. "… it definitely is, but when it comes time to leave him there, neither of us will be able to hold it together. In fact, the very thought of it makes me…" Elle burst into tears and her older sister immediately wrapped an arm around her to comforted her. Although tears formed in her eyes as well, Anne did not cry, she did not blubber, she did not sob. She was her father's daughter, and as he had always taught her, she could not cry until the problem was solved.

So Anne stoically sat there with her arm around her little sister, telling her it was all right. Yes, it was all right

194

to just let it out. She said it in a calm and reassuring voice and kissed her sibling on the top of her head, not giving the slightest indication that emotionally she felt as though she were trapped inside a fiery airplane plummeting from the sky.

Chapter 26

An hour later, both Anne and Elle were strolling through the grass in the back yard trying to come to terms with their decision to place their father in hospice. As they walked, Elle noticed it needed mowing. "Yeah," Anne replied giving the area the once over. "I'll take care of it a little later."

Elle stopped and took her sister's arm. "So what *did* Dad freak out about yesterday?"

Anne's face tightened. "It was the Luke thing."

Elle huffed and looked away, clearly annoyed. "I never understood why Bob thought it necessary to hide his leukemia treatments from Dad those first few months. How could he be so brilliant, yet be so stupid as to use that bullshit line about wanting to spend time with his buddy 'Luke' as a cover?" Elle shook her head. "Did he think that was witty? Damn it! I'm so pissed that he dragged us into it. Especially when Dad discovered that we knew about Bob's illness all along."

Anne nodded in exasperation. "Boy, that **was** a horror show! I'll never forget Dad's expression during Bob's funeral when he asked us if we thought 'Luke' might show up to pay his respects."

Elle's lips became a thin red line. "Yeah! He–who–takes-no-shit can be pretty damn vindictive at times."

Anne then relayed the story Mrs. Tuttle told her.

Elle stopped and momentarily stared off. "Yeah, I can see why you say we have no choice. I shudder to think what might have happened had Dad gotten out of the house." She turned to her sister. "I know it might sound crazy but so far all of Dad's delusions have had a basis in fact. Remember Mrs. Tuttle's Jim Beau's analogy?

"Yes, but Dad's clearly getting worse. The new meds may be cutting down his excursion time, but the episodes are more frequent and more frightening."

As they resumed walking Elle let out a sigh, exhaled and said, "Well, to add to the party atmosphere let me just mention that another problem has reared its ugly head."

Anne turned to face her sister. "Really?!? Unbelieveable!" After shaking her head, she said, "Okay, let's have it."

Elle slid her hands under the hem of the bulky sweater and into her pockets. "While I was in Manhattan yesterday, I got a call yesterday from a headhunter. One of the biggest. They said one of Goldenrod's competitors has a position open and they were especially interested in talking with me." Elle took a calming breath to settle down. Lately new challenges were coming faster than she could sort them out.

"Knowing that Elliot is a vindictive prick, and suspecting the call might be a trap, instead of calling back, I walked over to the headhunters offices and asked to speak to the woman who called."

"And?"

Elle smirked. "It turns out the call was legit. World Traveler, the biggest of all the hotel chains has been following my career since I became Senior V.P. When they read that I had been tapped to head Great Ex, they made a counteroffer. And a VERY lucrative one, I might add. AND one that will very likely put me in the CEO chair in three years. Which is something that will never happen as long as Elliot, with his constant sniping and badmouthing my management style, is at the helm at Goldenrod."

197

Anne began kicking at the fallen leaves as they walked. "Interesting. So what's the plan? Are you going to take the offer?"

Elle reached down and plucked a pretty blue flower from a bush and placed it behind her ear. "I'm seriously considering it, but, there is the matter of health insurance. One very good thing about Goldenrod is they allow non-married employees to select one additional person to be covered on their medical insurance. So I put Dad on mine. World Traveler doesn't offer that. Which means if I leave Goldenrod, Dad loses his coverage."

"Ahh, crap. So what are you going to do?"

Elle sighed. "I'm not sure. I have a Linked-In connection who is a major player in the health insurance field. I'll drop him a line and see if he can offer some advice."

Chapter 27

As Anne and Eleanor walked the expanse of their back yard, Jim had taken a seat on the edge of his bed and pressed his hands to his temples.

Good heavens, how much did I drink last night? he asked himself. *I can't remember ever having a hangover this bad. It feels like someone drove a railroad spike into my skull.*

He staggered to the door on his way to the bathroom to get some aspirin. He jiggled the knob. The door was locked.

"Hello?" he called out. "Hello?!" this time a little louder. "Is anybody home? Can anybody hear me?"

As he began pounding on the door, Mrs. Tuttle entered the house with the prescription and an armful of groceries. She heard Jim banging and called out. "Hold your horses! I'm coming, I'm coming!"

After dropping the groceries and meds on the kitchen table, she scooted down the hall to Jim's room, key in hand.

As she opened the door, Jim said, "Thank you, Mrs. Tuttle."

She looked him over and asked, "How are you feeling?"

"Like I got kicked in the head," he said grimacing. "I can't remember ever having a hangover this bad. Must have gotten really plowed last night. No wonder you locked me in my room. The aspirin (hic) is still in the medicine cabinet? (hic) Aww great, now I got the hic (hic) cups."

As Jim cautiously made his way to the bathroom with his hand pressed against the wall, Mrs. Tuttle went out the

199

back and trotted toward the girls. When they saw her approaching, they picked up their pace to meet her.

"Your father's awake," the caregiver called out as the daughters drew closer.

"How's he doing?" Anne called back.

Now just a few yards away and slowing, she replied, "He thinks he has a bad hangover. I didn't correct him because I was concerned he'd feel bad about having another episode."

Eleanor eyed her sister. "Mrs. Tuttle has a point. Since we're placing him in hospice anyway, I see no reason to tell him what really happened. That will just upset him."

Anne turned to Mrs. Tuttle. "Does he seem all right? I mean, is he clear-headed? I don't want to drop the hospice bomb if he's not going to remember it."

Mrs. Tuttle fell in step alongside them as they headed to the house. "He seems lucid enough, but that doesn't mean he'll gonna stay that way." She paused and then said, "So you've decided to go ahead with your hospice plans. Frankly, I think it's the right move. With him phasing in and out at a moment's notice, he needs round the clock care."

"Yes, "Anne said. "It seems like the right time. He requires more care than the three of us can give him."

"When is he being admitted?"

"I'm going to call Ms. Paris now and see when a bed will be available. Once that's established, I'll tell Dad the news."

"Maybe we ought to take Dad there for a look around first," Eleanor suggested as the three climbed the back deck stairs. "See if he likes it. If not, we can show him other places."

Anne shook her head. "The situation is complicated enough. I'll call NorthCountry and see how soon he can be admitted. You get a hold of your Linked-In buddy and iron out the insurance issues. Regardless, he's going to hospice and he's going as soon as humanly possible," she said sternly. "In his present condition he's likely to do something that we can't handle or drag some other poor hapless soul into the August family horror show."

"But…" Eleanor said.

"No buts, Elle," Anne snapped. "This has to be done and there's no sense delaying it. The time has come to put this issue to bed once and for all.

*

Just as Jim was about to open the medicine cabinet, he caught a glimpse of his face and his heart sank. To say he looked terrible would be a compliment. His eyes were bloodshot and his lower lids sagged. His complexion was blotchy, and there were deep wrinkles he had never noticed before.

(Hic)

Good Lord, I look like something dragged out of the bottom of a pyramid!

(Hic)

"Damn it!" he shouted and drew in a deep breath to hopefully stop the hiccupping.

After thirty seconds or so with no hiccups, he started breathing normally again and reached for the aspirin. The label read **Triple-Strength** in huge colorful letters and Jim sincerely hoped they weren't kidding because he felt like his head was going to blow off his shoulders. He quickly shook four out of the plastic bottle and was about to slide one back in, when he said, "The hell with it," and popped

201

all four into his mouth. He grabbed the bathroom glass, filled it with water and washed them down.

Returning the glass to the center of the toothbrush rack and the aspirin bottle to the medicine cabinet, he placed his hands on the rim of the sink and decided to stay right there until the pain subsided or his head blew off. Either way was fine with him.

He closed his eyes and drew a breath.

(Hic)

"Aww, shit!"

(Hic)

Five minutes later, noting that his hiccups had stopped and his headache was easing, he opened his eyes, drew a breath and said, "Yeah, that's better. Much better." He pressed the heel of his hand to his forehead and pressed it over the spot where the pain had been. It was a dull ache now and was quickly subsiding.

He breathed a sigh of relief, then up to the mirror to see if he looked any better, figuring *any* change would likely be an improvement.

Then he saw it.

On the mirror written in soap were the words. ***Pop-Pop where are you? You said you were coming to get me. Please hurry, I hurt so bad.***

Bosco O'Bama the Third.

Anna was on the phone, Eleanor on the Internet and Mrs. Tuttle was preparing lunch when they heard Jim call out in panic from the bathroom.

Eleanor, Smartphone in hand, rushed in with Mrs. Tuttle right behind her. Jim pointed to the mirror in gap-lawed shock.

202

"How did that get there?! he asked turning to them. "I was in here the whole time and that wasn't on the mirror when I came in."

Eleanor leaned out the door and called to her sister to join them. Anne, deeply engaged in conversation stuck up her index finger to indicate she needed a minute.

"I was standing right here in this very spot," he said pointing, to the floor. He pressed his hand to his head and paced. "Could this be some kind of sick magic trick? You know, like that street magician guy who throws water at a wall and the name of the person they're thinking of appears?"

Mrs. Tuttle shook her head. "You wrote it."

Jim spun toward her. "I wrote it?"

She pointed at the mirror. "That's your handwriting. You leave reminder notes all over the house. I'd recognize that double-crossed **t** anywhere.

He turned back to the mirror, then sank back against the wall and ran his hands through his hair. "You're right. That is my handwriting. It must have written it. But when? I don't remember writing it."

Anne walked in, took a look at the mirror and said. "That's because you were on one of your excursions when you did it."

Jim stared at her agape. "But how? I was here the entire time. Right here on this very spot."

Anne's expression indicated that she believed him, but then explained, "You may have been physically here but your mind was off exploring. You can tell by the signature. Bosco only exists in your fantasy place. The doctor did say the new meds would lessen the time of your excursions but it seems they're coming more often."

Jim staggered over and sat on the closed toilet lid. "So I did write it!" He pressed his hands to the sides of his head. "That's really unsettling! That I could do something like that and not know it."

Anne stepped over to him and placed a comforting hand on his shoulder. "Dad, Eleanor and I have discussed it and we think you should be admitted to hospice like we discussed. It's... time, Dad. You don't have a hangover, at least not the type you think. Mrs. Tuttle had to heavily sedate you because you were experiencing a... well, let's call a spade a spade... a psychotic episode."

Jim pressed his palm to his face. "Dear Lord..."

"It's a beautiful place, Dad," Anne said as she sat on the rim of the bathtub. "Top-of-the-line everything. Doctors, nurses, attendants, dieticians, you name it. Good, healthy food and medication monitoring. And we'll visit every weekend."

Jim nodded and stood. "I'm sure it will be fine. The decision had to be made and I'm glad it's done." He turned to Mrs Tuttle. "I'm going to miss our go-rounds but thank you. You've been a godsend. Before I go, I'll write you a proper reference."

He turned back to Anne. "So, when do we leave?"

Anne stood, placed her hands behind her back, looked her father straight in the eye and in an emotionally filled voice said, "Tomorrow morning... 10 o'clock."

Jim drew a breath and straightened his shoulders. "I'll be ready. In the meantime, I'll be in my room." With that, Jim gently pressed past Ms. Tuttle and Eleanor and made his way out.

Although it was barely midafternoon, the blinds in Jim's room were pulled closed, giving it a twilight, and almost ethereal appearance. All his personal items and daily necessities were in black and white and shades of gray.

He carefully surveyed the room. It looked somewhat alien to him now. He had slept in this room for decades, first with his wife, then later alone. He had replaced the furniture, as well as everything else—pictures, rugs, tables, chairs, lamps and photographs—not wanting anything to remind him of their bitter breakup. It was sparsely furnished now. Gone were the items that had given it a woman's touch and sense of style. Just a bed, end table, lamps, mirror, desk, a couple of chairs, and a few photographs of him and his daughters. Those of his son and those taken of his family before the breakup had been stored away in the attic, with the one exception of Bob's photo on the mantle in the living room.

So this is how it ends. Not with a bang but with a whimper.

He clasped his hands behind his back and began pacing.

This is the last day. The last day I'll be in my home with my family. The last day of my freedom. The last day to come and go as I please and make my own decisions.

My last day as a man.

Chapter 28

An hour later, Anne finished both mowing the lawn, and stacking items she had selected for disposal from the garage. With her father going to hospice, she and Elle would likely sell the house and put aside the money in case it was needed for Jim's continued care. The items being thrown out were mostly old toys from their childhood that were either rusted, worn out or ragged.

Elle joined her sister as she placed the items against the fence to be taken to the curb on trash day. Handing her a can of Arizona iced tea, she helped Anne roll out the metal barrel they used each autumn to burn leaves, broken and snapped branches, and other flammable debris that routinely littered the yard as the winter months approached.

Once collected and tossed in, Elle took her cigarette lighter, lit one of the dried branches and dropped it into the barrel. Within minutes, flames leapt from the rim and dying embers floated upon a blanket of warm currents.

Walking over and taking a seat on the deck steps, Elle, pulled what was now *her* cable-knit sweater tightly around her, turned to Anne and said, "You know this is illegal, right?"

Anne came over and sat beside her, then smirked and shrugged dismissively, "Yeah? So call a cop."

Elle chuckled, opened her pocket book, and rummaged for a piece of Nicorette gum. Finally finding one, she popped it out of the wrapper and tossed it into her mouth.

"Those things work?" Anne asked as she brushed the sweat from her brow, then leaned back, snapped open the can and took a sip of iced tea.

Elle paused, tilted her head, twisted her lips, then said, "Yeah, they do. It's not easy, but having the gum makes it possible to survive the cravings, which get pretty brutal, especially when you're trying to juggle a promotion, a merger, a job offer and putting one's father into hospice."

She placed her elbows on her knees, her chin on her hands and said, "Speaking about juggling things, still questioning your decision to become a cop?"

Anne gave a quick shake of her head. "No, that decision's been made. I'm done with law enforcement."

Elle studied her sibling. "Really!? Don't you think you should mull it around a little more? Consider your options?"

"It's a done deal," Anne replied, taking another sip. "You need a certain mindset to be an effective police officer. You need to be sharp, quick-witted, stable and committed to the job. I'm not that person anymore."

With a dismissive smirk, Elle said, "Bullshit! You're the most stable, clear-thinking person I know. You never panic, which is something I really love about you, sis, and you have more guts than a Navy SEAL."

Several seconds went by before Anne replied, "I saw the dashcam video of the shootout. At first I was impressed with how I handled it. Cool, calm, and professional. Then came the moment of truth when the gunman leaps from the car and holds his gun to that little girls head, and her sister cries out, 'Please don't kill my sister!'" And in that very moment, in that split second when facing the choice to drop my gun and very possibly get myself killed, or taking that second to shoot him in his head..."

Following a deep sigh Anne said, "And that's when I lost it. Killing that guy in that split second, taking that shot

207

and succeeding when I could have missed or hit the girl instead, caused me to... I don't know, freak out? Panic?

Another deep breath. "The video showed a crazed look on my face when I grabbed the dead guy's gun and started firing it, along with my own, into the driver. According to ballistics and the tape, I fired seventeen rounds into that guy over a period of twelve seconds."

Elle snarled. "And he disserved every damn one of them!"

After several swallows of iced tea, Anne continued. "I told Tremaine I kept firing because I knew I had been hit and was afraid that if I succumbed to my injuries, the remaining gunman, if he was also wearing a vest, would again use the children as human shields, or kill them. So I couldn't take that chance."

Elle made a fist and shook it. "Which is absolutely true!"

"Maybe. But it hadn't occurred to me at the time! My brain just froze, and I couldn't stop firing until I was out of bullets."

"Even if that IS true," Elle said dismissively, "that sonavabitch was shooting at you too, so you had every right to make sure he was dead."

"Again, maybe," Anne said as she rested her elbows on her thighs and gazed at the flames, "But I think the real reason was because I was frightened. No," she added, shaking her head and flinging her hands into the air, "I was scared out of my mind. I had never killed anyone before and had never been in a situation where I could get killed. So in raw panic, I kept pulling the trigger."

She paused for a moment then looked at her sister and said, "Ever see those videos when, as a prank, one guy dresses up in a monster costume and leaps out at his

208

unsuspecting friend and the friend, instead of squealing in panic, punches the guy in the face then beats the crap out him? I think that's what happened to me. Some people squeal in panic; others start swinging. To be an effective cop you can't do either. And so it's time to turn in my badge and gun and start looking at other careers."

"Wow!" Elle said, clearly stunned. "Boom, just like that!" She flung her hands apart to imitate an explosion. She then smiled, placed her arm around her sister's shoulder, pulled her close and said, "Well, you won't have to look long. Once I get settled in my new position I'll hire you and put you on the fast track to the corner office."

Anne patted her sister's hand and said, "That's sweet of you, hon, but I'm going to need a little time to figure out what it is I really what to do with my life. Still, I appreciate the offer."

Elle kissed her sister on the cheek and stood. "Well, I hope you find what you're looking for. C'mon, let's put the lawn mower and rakes back in the garage and start loading the car with Dad's things. By the looks of that sky, we're in for a storm."

Following Mrs. Tuttle's hourly check, it was the click of the closing door that woke Jim. Before laying down for a quick nap, he had packed two suitcases of clothes, plus his toiletries, and was ready for tomorrow's move.

He rose, opened the blinds, turned and saw the sun's reflection on the brass posts at the foot of his bed. He took a seat and scanned the room. On the bookshelf were several books, classics actually, that he had collected over the years and intended to read, but never did. On his laptop were several files he intended to save to a flash

209

drive, but had never gotten around to. Partial e-mails written to old friends he intended… but…

Where did the time go? How did I get this old? I feel my life has barely started and now suddenly, I'm at the end of the line.

Jim gave the room another cursory look, then noticed strange shadows dancing upon the walls. He turned from his place at the foot of the bed and in the window saw flickering red and yellow lights. He sprang to his feet and looked outside.

He staggered back in shock.

Whateverland was on fire!

Chapter 29

While cleaning out the garage, Anne's cell rang. The caller ID showed Tremaine's number. The possibility of impending bad news brought the anxiety lightning strikes back to her stomach. She considered letting it go to voicemail but couldn't. She had spent a lifetime tackling problems head on and was incapable of doing it any other way.

"Hello, Scott," Anne said, using her best pleasant voice. "I assume you have some news?"

"Well, it's more of an update. Actually, a good update," Scott replied. "I've just been informed that Mrs. Blanchet's lawyer has dropped out, citing case overload. The firm's other lawyers are using that excuse as well."

Anne was puzzled. As she strolled over to her father's workbench she said, "That's odd. I've never heard of that happening, especially in a civil suit that has potential billables in the millions. Any idea why?"

Scott chuckled, clearly excited to be relaying this news. "Oh, I *know* the real reason. When they first saw the video, they thought the case was a slam dunk, but afterward, when they saw the bullet holes in your car and windows, the damage to your vest, the X-rays of your broken ribs, the picture of the dead father killed execution style, AND heard the cleaned-up audio of the gunman's threat and the little girl's plea... Well, that certainly caused them to rethink their position. Also, the courthouse lawyers' cars rarely get ticketed, even though they often park in tow-away zones. It's a professional courtesy. At least it *was*. When word got out that they were suing you and the department after you had single-handedly saved the Blanchet family, the gloves came off.

211

"Top of the line BMWs, Mercedes Benz, Audis, Lexuses, Cadallacs, Lincolns, etc., were towed, paperwork lost, fines doubled, storage fees enacted, code violations found, you name it, they got ticketed for it." Scott chuckled again. "And since the lawyers *not* involved in the case wouldn't see a penny in settlement, and were convinced a jury would undoubtedly side with a female police officer who risked her life to save a young girl and her family, you can bet some intense pressure was placed on that firm to reconsider and chase their ambulances elsewhere."

"Hmm," Anne said, surprised at how things had worked out. "You think some other firm might take the case?"

Scott's enthusiasm cooled. "It's possible. But if it does, it will likely be a small firm with lawyers inexperienced in civil cases. They'd be eaten alive. So it looks like you're off the hook, at least for a while, and very likely for good. Oh, by the way, how's your dad doing?"

Anne sighed and leaned against the garage wall. "Not so good. We're having him admitted to hospice tomorrow. It's… it's time. We love him, but his illness has become more than we can handle. He needs round-the-clock professional care."

There was a pause, then Scott said, "I'm sorry to hear that. Have you decided what you're going to do once your suspension is lifted?"

"No, not yet," Anne said, now anxious to get off the phone. "I'll let you know once I do. But I have to go now. Got to get Dad ready. Do you need to talk to Eleanor?"

"No, no," he replied. "We'll catch up at the office."

212

Eleanor eyed her sister inquisitively as Anne shook her head. "Okay then," she said. "Good-bye," and ended the call. Anne placed her cell into her pocket. "Looks like I'm off the hook, at least for a while."

"That's good news. What did he say?"

As Anne relayed the story, neither sister noticed their father charging out of the house and into the yard.

Chapter 30

Jim could feel the wind press against his face as he and his mighty steed, Tally-Ho, raced through Whateverland on way to the Land o' Jungles to make sure all the animals were safe and not trapped by the approaching flames. He could see the dying embers floating by as distant flames and smoke devoured the streets and arcade amusements of Land o' the Midway.

Bosco's going to be so disappointed.

And there was also his concern for Bosco. Fortunately, the Rest Area where Luke had imprisoned the boy was at the far end of the park and close to the lake. If necessary, they could wade into the water until the inferno burned itself out.

As Jim and Tally-Ho entered Land o' Jungles, they came upon an alligator leaning against a tree smoking a cigar. It was Wally the Gator, by far the laziest of all Whateverland's creatures. "Hey there, Hopalong," he said as Jim approached. "What's all the hubbub, bub?"

Jim pulled the reins taut and the mighty steed slowed to a halt. "Look around, chucklehead," he shouted as he motioned to the surrounding area. "Whateverland is on fire. You need to follow me to safety."

Wally held up his clawed hand and said, "Whoa, let's not be hasty, I've got a fine Cuban cigar here and..."

Jim was in no mood to listen, instead, he reached down, grabbed Wally by the scruff and placed him behind him on the horse.

"Tally-Ho! Tally-Ho," Jim cried out, as he spurred his mighty stallion into action. He turned to Wally. "Where are the rest of the animals?"

214

"Most are gone," Wally replied, blowing out a plume of fine Cuban cigar smoke. "Followed Gladys and those pain-in-the-ass monkeys to the Indian territories. The few that are left were heading toward the Great Wall of Whateverland. At least they were when I last saw them."

Panic washed over Jim's face. "The Great Wall? Good Lord, the fire is heading that way. We've got to go back and save them!"

"Are you crazy?" Wally asked, placing his head on Jim's shoulder. "We'd never get past the flames! Tell you what—let's head to the lake and come back later. By then, they should be nicely barbequed and quite tasty."

"That's not funny!" Jim said. "Those animals are our friends, and as the owner of Whateverland it's my responsibility to get them to safety!"

"Yeah? Well, then, you go right ahead, but as for me... well, whatdoyaknow! This is my stop. Ta-ta!" With that Wally the Gator slid off Tally-Ho's back and onto the ground.

Jim turned, and saw that Wally landed just fine. He considered going back and grabbing him, but realized he needed the room to get the other animals to safety.

The flames grew higher and more powerful as he rode to save his woodland friends. Moments later, he felt the first few sprinkles of rain but doubted even a heavy downpour could douse this inferno. Continuing to risk life and limb, he dodged falling branches and walls of fire and smoke.

At one point he thought it was a lost cause. *No animal can survive these flames*, he told himself. But as he was about to turn around, he heard cries for help, coming from the Great Wall of Whateverland.

215

Quoting Rosencrantz, Jim shouted, "Into the breach!" and as lightning crackled and thunder roared, he and Tally-Ho charged into the fires.

*

"Wow! That last thunderclap was pretty loud!" Elle said pressing her hands to her ears.

She and Anne were in the back of the garage, sorting through the items, and deciding what they should keep and what they should toss.

Anne looked out the open garage door. "The fire inside the barrel is getting pretty big, and the metal is starting to glow. Think I should hit it with the hose?"

Elle joined her sister and looked out. "Nah, it's starting to rain. After a few minutes, the barrel will cool down and the smoke will disappear."

The door that led from the garage to the house opened and Mrs. Tuttle stuck her head in. "I'm leaving now. I made some sandwichs and left them on the table, should you want a quick snack. Also, I checked on your father a few minutes ago. He was asleep, although he will likely be getting up pretty soon. You may want to give him another look if you're going to stay out here for a while."

"Just leave that door open, Mrs. Tuttle," Elle said. "If he leaves his room we'll come inside."

Anne approached. "We'll use your van to take Dad tomorrow, and afterward I'll write your severance check."

Mrs. Tuttle nodded, indicating that was fine with her, then said her good-byes and headed out.

Anne turned and said, "Elle? I'm going to go through the stuff over here." She pointed to the collected items. "This way should Dad get up and start wandering around, I'll hear him and make sure he doesn't get into trouble."

216

"Works for me," Elle said as she flung a broken rake handle out the garage doorway. It ricocheted against the bottom of the metal barrel creating a hole in the rusted metal. Flames immediately poured from it and Elle became concerned the old rusted barrel might fall apart and spread its flames to the garage.

She was about to voice her concerns to Anne, when she saw rainwater pouring furiously from the rain gutters and drainpipes and make its way to the barrel's growing flames.

As Jim and Tally-Ho raced through the smoke and fire toward the cries for help, a tree branch snapped and fell to the ground before the wall of flame. There was a thunderous crash and Tally-Ho reared up on her hind legs.

"Easy girl, easy!" Jim said stroking the steed's golden mane.

Tally-Ho turned, faced him and said. "Easy my ass! That branch nearly took my head off! You still think this rescue mission is a good idea?"

"What would *your* answer be if you were among those crying for help?" Jim asked.

Tally-Ho thought for a moment, chuffed, shook her head and said. "Ah, balls! All right. Let's do this."

After maneuvering around the trees and hot spots, Jim and Tally-Ho saw the remaining animals of Whateverland trapped against the Great Wall with no room to escape the approaching flames.

They quickly surveyed the area trying to find a way in to rescue Tony Tiger, Opus the Penguin, Yogi the Bear, Donald the Duck, Bugs the Bunny and Moria the giant ancient turtle. But the wall of flame before them appeared impenetrable.

There came a roar in the distance, amid the heavy rain Jim turned and saw a wall of water rushing toward them. "Tally-Ho," he said, "the Whaverland dam's flood gates must have opened to relieve the pressure. We must get our friends to high ground or we'll all be swept away. We'll have to leap over the flames, grab our friends and charge up the hill before the waters engulf us."

Tally-Ho, seeing the approaching threat, realized there were no other options. "Okay, Jim," she said. "But I'm going to have to gallop faster than I've ever galloped before so you had better hold on tight because if you fall off, you're on your own and will likely wind up as Wally's barbeque dinner."

With that said, she took off. Moved so fast that Jim was barely able to breathe. But he held tight as Tally-Ho ran faster still. Before them was the tower of fire with its flames licking the very sky. This was the moment of truth, either they succeeded or all was lost.

At a speed never reached before, Tally-Ho leapt into the air and she and Jim soared into the sky and over the flames. Just as it appeared they were home free, Jim's foot struck something and suddenly flames were all around them!

"What the hell was that?" Anne asked as she turned to her sister who was removing an old sled from it's hooks on the back wall.

"Give me a second," Elle grunted as she finally managed to pull the wooden sled down and drop it on the garage floor. "There! I though those rusted hooks were never going to come loose."

Feeling satisfied, she turned looked outside and saw the old metal barrel had toppled over and its flaming

218

contents were being doused by the heavy rainfall and the spewing drainpipes. Although still very much on fire, it wouldn't be too long before the water put it out.

"Oh well," Eleanor said, placing her hands on her hips and surveyed the situation. "Looks like the old barrel finally gave up the ghost. She sniffed. "Just as well I guess. It had outlived its usefulness. Might as well wait until the fire's out and the metal cools down before we start cleaning it up."

"What did we hit?" Tally-Ho asked as they raced into the forest toward the Great Wall of Whateverland.

"I'm not sure," Jim replied. "But it hurt my foot pretty good."

"My hoof as well," Tally-Ho replied. "The fog's getting pretty thick. It becoming difficult to see ahead. Any better view from up there?"

"No, but I remember this path we're on. It leads to the great wall. Pick up the pace, if you can, Tally, that tower of flame may have slowed the waters but I'm sure it hasn't stopped them."

"That's odd," Elle commented as she stood at the edge of garage doorway, studying the tipped over barrel and the dying flames.

"What's odd?" Anne asked coming up alongside.

Elle gestured to the barrel. "I thought the base of the barrel cracked from the heat and that's what caused it to fall over but the base is still in one piece. So why did it tip over?"

Anne shivered slightly. "Don't know, don't care. All I know is that I'm getting wet from all this stream. So enough of this, I got stuff to do.

219

She turned and headed back with her younger sibling soon to follow.

With the fog disapating, Jim and Tally-Ho made it to the Great Wall of Whateverland and after making room for their woodland friends on the back of Tally-Ho, they all galloped off enroute to the Rest Area where Bosco was being held.

The rain fell steadily, drenching Jim and the animals amid frequent bursts of thunder and lightning. Most of the animals wanted to take shelter and wait out the storm but Jim immediately vetoed the idea. He was their leader, had resued them all and wasn't going to stop until Bosco was free from the grip of that psychopath, Luke.

He had formed a plan. When they reached the Rest Area entrance, he would dismount Tally-Ho and instruct her to take the animals to Whateverland Lake where Cissy the Blue Whale would ferry them to safety.

As for Jim, this was game time. That bastard Luke hurt his beloved grandson Bosco O'Bama the Third, and he would not let that stand. This monster needed to be dealt with. And yes, he knew he would be facing Luke in his own territory. (He hadn't forgotten the graffiti that read, *HERE, LUKE RULES!*) Nor had he forgotten the bugs that stung and left him with an increasingly painful left arm and upper left torso. Not that it mattered now. This battle wasn't between Bosco and Luke, this battle was between Luke and him.

But Jim always somehow suspected that. Luke had figured out that the things that brought joy into Jim's life ended long ago. The old man no longer cared about fame and fortune. He had them both and they brought little comfort. He had been loved by millions, but it had been a

220

predatory love. The kind of love that causes your so-called devotees to hang from the sides of your ambulance like they did Michael Jackson's, hoping to film your final moments and death rattle.

He once had a family but its matriarch plotted against him and tried to destroy all he had created.

And through it all, Jim had been stoic and uncompromising, refusing to show weakness or fear.

But Luke had found his Achilles' heel and clearly intended to use that one weak spot to inject as much misery and heartache as the old man could stand.

And he would likely succeed.

But it would come at a price. A very high price.

Jim August would see to that.

Chapter 31

When Jim and his animal companions reached the fork in the road, it was raining heavily. However, the time had come for goodbyes and farewells. All involved knew this would be their last time together.

As Jim dismounted, he said, "Here's what we're going to do. Tally-Ho, you and the others continue on to the lake while I tend to my grandson. Once you're there, Cissy will take you all to safety. Everybody understand?"

When he didn't receive a response, Jim, momentarily puzzled said, "Well, speak up, what do you think of my plan?"

Tony Tiger said, "Grrreeeeaaaaaattttt!" Bugs the Bunny said, "Sounds good to me, doc." Billy the Cat said "Ack!" Moria the giant turtle said "Not that it matters." And nobody could make out what Donald the Duck said. However it was clear they were all on board and following the tearful goodbyes from all involved, Tally-Ho and her woodland companions rode off for the lake.

*

As Anne swept the floor of the garage and was bending down to collect the dirt, she suddenly jerked up. "Oh, crap! I forgot to cover the toys and stuffed animals alongside the fence with a tarp. If those stuffed animals got soaked..." She immediately searched for something to cover them.

When Elle found the blue tarp they sometimes used to cover the cars when a big snowfall was expected, Anne took it and raced to the fence.

But when she got there, the stuffed animals were gone.

Holding the tarp over her head, she said, "I know I brought the stuffed animals out here with the other..."

222

A startling thought struck her. She dropped the tarp and raced up the deck stairs and into the house.

"Dad! Dad?" she called out. When she received no answer, she said, "Damn it!" She ran to his bedroom, knocked, then burst in and surveyed the empty room.

"Aww, shit!"

She ran to the front door and finding it locked, heaved a sigh of relief. At least he hadn't left the property. She grabbed the two umbrellas from the umbrella stand and charged toward the garage. Once inside, she said, "Dad's on the loose." She tossed her sister an umbrella.

"How did he get out? We were here the whole time!" Elle said, catching it.

Anne shrugged, stepped to the garage door and opened her umbrella. "I'll take the left, you take the right. We'll meet at the end of the tall brush by the atrium."

The thought that her father may have ventured into the brush and could have gone as far as the spring water atrium at the very end of their property deeply concerned Elle and her sister. Both women agreed never to mow the grass at the back third so that it was a chore to lumber through. They figured the more difficult the journey, the less likely their father would come upon the spring water atrium and possibly drown.

Of course, there was the other issue out there.

"Damn it, damn it, damn it!" Anne growled in frustration as she set out into the rain and the left side of their property. Elle opened her umbrella and set out toward the right muttering the stronger expletive, "Shit, shit, shit!"

As Jim entered the Rest Area, he turned and saw that the heavy downpour was slowly, but effectively, putting

223

out the fire. The waters arrived far too late however. Whateverland was in ruins. The Land o' the Midway was totally destroyed, as were the amusements, games and rides. The Land o' Jungles was empty now that all the animals had moved on to greener and safer pastures. And as for the Land o' the Future, well, as Rosencrantz had said, it was as if it had never existed.

But Jim couldn't dwell on these things. The only thing that mattered was getting Bosco O'Bama the Third away from Luke and to a safe haven.

And that he would do. Regardless of cost.

His first mistake was that he hadn't properly prepared for the bugs. As he trudged through the muck and the dead trees and ugly landscape he was again stung and a lightning bolt of pain raced through his left arm, knocking the breath out of him.

He leaned against a tree for a minute to steady himself and catch his breath. Once done, he resumed his quest, marching forward to rescue his grandson and make Luke pay for what he'd done.

Minutes later, he saw a figure in the deep shadows. Jim stopped and eyed him.

"I was wondering when you'd finally get here," a voice called out. It was a powerful voice, but not powerful in strength or resonance. Rather it was powerful in the way one would describe a stench or foul odor. He added, "I was beginning to think you'd forgotten about us."

"Step forward and show yourself!" Jim called out. There came another thunderbolt of pain in his left arm but he refused to acknowledge it. "Face me, you coward! And stop harming children when it's the adult you're after."

Luke's reply was a cold, cruel laugh as he slowly approached. "Don't be absurd. How better to rip out a

224

chunk of a parent's soul than to slowly and mercilessly torture their child *while... they... watch*?"

"To hell with you!" Jim growled, then turned and pushed toward the giant beam of light. As he drew closer he called out, "Bosco! It's Pop-Pop. Can you hear me? Where are you?"

Pushing through the dense bushes and wild foliage and almost upon the light itself, he spotted a marker. As he drew closer, he realized that it was a tombstone.

As he bent down to read it, his left arm screamed in pain.

His voice soon followed.

*

The scream stopped Anne in her tracks. On the other side of the property it had the same effect on Eleanor. Both women now knew exactly where it was coming from and

likely why he screamed.

They charged toward the sound.

*

In excruciating pain and with watery eyes, Jim looked to his side and saw a sword had been run through his left arm, then pulled out.

As Jim turned and staggered to his feet, Luke stood before him holding the bloodied weapon. Now in plain sight, Jim studied the figure. He was tall and clearly ancient, all muscle and sinew, low brow, thick eyebrows, and deep set eyes. His head was misshapen, like a poorly formed lump of clay; his skin thick and covered with scales. "Well, what did you think I was going to do?" Luke asked. "Just allow you to storm into MY kingdom and release MY prisoner?" He grinned. "Just what kind of monster would I be if I allowed that?" His grin grew ever

225

wider. "Now that you're here I'm going to make Bosco watch as I make *you* suffer! Take you apart piece by piece just like I did…

He didn't get to finish that sentence.

*

It didn't take long before the two sisters joined up and raced side by side to the far end of the property. Anne noticed her sister's troubled expression and said, "I know what you're thinking." She took a hard swallow. "But if he's at the gravestone, that scream means he's still alive."

*

The pain didn't matter. The wound didn't matter. That Whateverland was in ruins didn't matter because everything had become bright red. Every emotion Jim possessed scrambled for cover as his white hot rage rocketed to the surface.

This bastard is talking about hurting my grandson? Going to torture me just to further upset him?!

Before Luke could finish the sentence, Jim's fist slammed into Luke's jaw with a fury and power the old man hadn't felt in years. Luke staggered backward, his face twisted in pain and confusion. Jim struck him again and again, knocking Luke to the ground then he jumped on his opponent's chest, pummeling Luke mercilessly. His unleashed fury fueled the power of every blow. "You think I'd let you hurt my grandson? You didn't think I'd make you pay?!?"

The old man hit him yet again, hard and to the bone but Luke's shock and confusion were fading. That cruel smirk again spread across his face.

"Not going to hurt your grandson?" he gasped and effortlessly pushed Jim off his chest. "Turn around, you stupid old fool and read the name on that tombstone! Go

226

on!" he said, pointing his sword to the headstone directly behind him. "Have a nice long look!" Luke attempted to climb to his feet but had suffered too many blows to the head. He took a step, then fell to the ground unconscious.

Jim rose to his feet with his heart pounding, his chest tightening. He approached the stone in pure terror and with an expression of pure terror, The moonlight illuminated the words.

Here Lies Bosco O'Bama the Third
Beloved son. Beloved brother.
Beloved friend.

Jim throat tightened and a thunderous pang of despair grew within him.

But… as he started at the inscription, the letters in the name began disappearing and rearranging.

Here Lies Bosco O'Bama the Third
Here's Lies Ro b t Boc O'Ba A u s ird
Here's Lies Robert "Bo 'B" Aug st
And finally: **Here's Lies Robert "BOB" August**
Beloved son. Beloved brother.
Beloved friend.

As Jim's jaw dropped in astonishment, Bosco O'Bama the Third stepped out from the shadows and with each step, he transformed from the loveable four-year-old boy and into the adult figure of Jim August's third child.

Bob.

Jim immediately threw his arms around his son and hugged him tightly. "Oh, dear God, Bob. I thought I'd never see you again."

*

"There he is!" Anne called out as both woman rushed to their father's side. He was lying unconscious with his

227

arms wrapped around their brother's tombstone, rainwater pouring from every fold in his jacket

Elle was first to reach him. She dropped to her knees and gently shook him.

There was no response.

Seeing this, Anne tossed her umbrella, bent down, ripped open his shirt and placed her ear against his chest. "He's in cardiac arrest. We need an ambulance!"

As Elle dialed 911, Anne began CPR.

*

As tears streamed from his eyes, Jim held his son at arm's length and studied him. "How? How is this possible?" he asked.

Bob patted his father on the shoulder and said, "I'll explain everything a little later, Pop. As for now, we need to get the hell out of here before Luke wakes up."

Jim snarled at their dazed and groggy assailant who was only now beginning to stir. "Yeah, well, I'm not afraid of him."

Bob took his father's arm and directed him toward the lake. "Well, you ought to be! I know from experience that he's not a creature to be trifled with."

Since his son seemed to have matters under control, Jim fell into lock step. "Where are we going?" he asked.

"To the lake," Bob replied. "I have a boat waiting, but he won't wait long if he sees Luke charging after us."

*

"The ambulance is on the way!" Elle said pacing nervously as her sister continued CPR. As Anne paused for a moment to listen to his heart, Elle said, "How's he doing? Is he going to be okay?" Anne looked up, her face was pale when she said, "I can't find a pulse," then resumed CPR.

228

*

As Bob and Jim neared the lake, the clouds above turned a menacing shade of black and swirled in predatory fashion. Jim felt like the strong winds were being blown directly into his lungs.

As father and son reached the shoreline, at the end of the dock was Cap'n Spaulding with Polly on his shoulder. The Cap'n was loosening the Charon's mooring ropes and momentarily stopped to frantically motion Jim and Bob to hurry.

He had good reason to be concerned. The ship was rocking wildly as the waters crashed against the dock. Water exploded in all directions as seagulls squawked and flapped their wings furiously to keep from being blown away. Thunder struck with such fury the arc lamps along the dock rattled. Walnut-sized hail began falling and each strike was like a rock hurled from the sky.

At one point the two men were literally hydroplaning across the dock way toward the choppy waters when Bob saw one of the mooring ropes snaking toward them. He grabbed it in midair, wrapped his arm around his father's waist, and the two pulled themselves toward the ship.

"Put your backs into it, men!" the Cap'n shouted above the shrieking winds. "If we're not a sea in the next few moments, they'll be no ship left to board!"

Inside the windowsill of the ship's cabin, Polly, wearing a yellow slicker similar to the Cap'n's, was pacing from side to side squawking, "Haul ass! Haul ass!"

Bob leapt into the rocking boat but slipped and fell on the soaked deck. Quickly righting himself, he grabbed the railing with one hand and pulled his father aboard with the other.

229

Now inside the cabin, Cap'n Spaulding fired up the engines as Polly flapped and leapt from one end of the cabin to the other squawking. "Warp speed, Mr. Sulu. Warp speed!"

As Bob opened and entered through the cabin door, Jim, still on deck turned to see Luke trotting up to the end of the pier.

"Old man!" he shouted above the roaring storm and crashing waves. "We have unfinished business!"

*

"Back here! Back here!" Elle yelled, jumping and waving to get the arriving Emergency Medical Technicians attention. Only minutes earlier the rain had stopped and she had run to the front gate, unlocked and opened it, knowing every second counted.

Now back at her father's side, she helped one EMT prepare his equipment, as Anne turned the CPR duties over to the other.

"We're going to need the paddles," the man giving Jim CPR said. "He's not responding."

*

As Cap'n Spaulding pulled the Charon from the dock and quickly increased speed, Luke stormed forward. "UNFINISHED BUSINESS!" he bellowed. He struck his sword to the wood below his feet until a bolt of lightning struck its hilt, then ricocheted and struck Jim directly in the chest.

*

Kyle studied the screen as his partner Warren pulled the paddles from Jim's chest. He shook his head. "Still no pulse. Reset."

*

230

As Jim staggered backward, he saw Bob in the window racing toward the cabin door. Jim threw his back against it and held it shut. "Stay inside!" he shouted to his son. "I won't let him get us both."

He winced as an arrow struck his left arm.

His back suddenly arched and his eyes nearly popped out of his head when a massive bolt of lightning struck Jim's chest again. But then... just for a second, he saw his two angels standing over him. Hands folded in prayer, gazing at him with loving concern.

"Ah. my angels!" he gasped with a smile. The angels faded and were soon gone.

Back at the pier's edge, Luke flung his bow to the ground and flailed wildly, stomping his feet and shrieking the words, "UNFINISHED BUSINESS!"

Jim smiled. Grinned actually. They were now out of Luke's reach, his enemy powerless. Amid Luke's fading and tormented cries, Jim knew all business between them was, at last, finished. With a smile, he closed his eyes, exhaled, slipped to the deck floor and let the darkness envelop him like a blanket.

*

Kyle shook his head as he stood and ran his sleeve against his brow. "I'm sorry, ladies. We did all we could do. Gave him a shot of adrenaline, performed CPR, and used the paddles. I'm afraid he's gone."

Elle pushed forward. "But I saw him open his eyes. Say, 'My Angels'. You saw him! He can't be dead!"

Kyle nodded and said, "Yes, I saw that, too. That's why we spent the last ten minutes trying to revive him. But his heart hasn't beat once since then, regardless of all our efforts."

Grief-stricken and shaking Elle said, "But..."

231

Anne took her arm and leaned in. "Elle… stop," she said gently. "Let him go. Think about it. If we brought him back, what would we be bringing him back to?"

Elle took a couple of short breaths, tried to form words, and when nothing came out bowed her head and sobbed.

Wrapping her arm around her younger sister, Anne thanked the EMTs as they removed the stretcher from the ambulance. She was about to return with Elle to the house when Elle stiffened and said, "Good Lord, I just figured it out!" She faced her sister. "Want to know who Bosco O'Bama the Third is?"

Before Anne could reply, Elle said, "Look at the tombstone and tell me what Bosco's initials are."

Anne's hand ran to her mouth. "Oh my goodness! It was Bob all along!"

Elle added, "And the Third referred to the fact Bob was the third child!"

*

As Jim stirred and opened his eyes, he soon realized he was sitting in a deck chair on Cap'n Spaulding's ship with Bob standing over him. "Hey there, Pop!" Bob said holding a cup of coffee. He gave it to his father. "I had it ready knowing you can't function until you've at least finished your first cup.

"Thanks," Jim replied. He sniffed the coffee, and the aroma was the most pleasant he had ever smelled. He took a sip and savored it.

Bob pulled over a green deck chair and sat down beside his father. "So, how are you doing? How do you feel?"

Jim took a breath. Moved his arms around a bit, then stood. He took another deep breath and said, "Actually,

232

I've never felt better." He checked his arm and noted that it was pain free and there had been no scaring. As he walked to the railing, sipping his coffee, he looked to the back of the boat and saw that the beam of light was now behind them.

At last, all the events of the past few days fell into place. For the first time in a year, everything made sense.

He turned to his son. "It wasn't a hallucination, was it? You were there the whole time, helping me through, guiding me over the rough spots."

Bob smiled and shrugged. "Well, maybe a little. Besides, turnabout is fair play, isn't it? You did it for me; you were by my side during every excruciating moment of my leukemia treatments. Always with an encouraging word; always with loving concern. I know the girls meant well, and did all they could, but not having gone through it themselves, they couldn't fully grasp what you were experiencing or the torment it brought. I could."

Jim took another sip of coffee. *Man! This is SO good!* "One question—why were you so suspicious of Cap'n Spaulding? I got the impression you thought he was trying to hurt me?"

Bob rose from his chair and joined his father at the rail. "Ahh, the ferryman. That's kind of difficult to explain. His job is to take us where we are supposed to go, and frankly he doesn't like waiting. And you and I gave him quite a delay when he came for me, so imagine how thrilled he must have been when he learned I was going back to help you through the transition."

Jim smiled. "So that's why he kept asking me if I wanted to go for a sail. He just wanted to get the job over with."

"Yeah, that's pretty much it," Bob said. "But all's well that ends well, right?"

"Right!" Jim replied.

As he looked over the calm waters and the soft blue skies, he saw a distant glimmer of stunningly beautiful colors. More vibrant and sharper than he had ever seen.

Jim finished his coffee and placed the empty cup on the table near his deck chair.

"Looking back, it wasn't all bad, you know," Jim said as he leaned against the deck railing. "I mean, the excursions. I don't think I was ever happier than when you and I were together in Whateverland. Riding our horses through Land o' Jungles, enjoying the rides and games in Land o' the Midway, eating ice cream and cotton candy."

Jim breathed in the salt air and said, "It may have only existed in my imagination, but I had some very happy times there. It was the place I always wished did exist. A place where I could look in any direction and see people happy and having fun. It was truly wonderful, and it broke my heart to see it destroyed."

Bob came over and placed his arm over his father's shoulder. "Dad, you don't fully understand how things work around here." Bob pointed over the railing, "See those colors out there on the horizon? See how much more beautiful and striking they are in comparison to the colors you're used to seeing?"

"They really are!" Jim replied.

"That applies to everything you've experienced so far." He directed Jim around the cabin and toward the ship's other side. "The Whateverland you imagined had to disappear to make way for the one that actually exists. You see, Pop, we all get the Whateverland we deserve.

234

And you..." Bob said as the two rounded the corner, "... have one of the grandest I have ever seen!"

With that, Bob directed his father's attention to the approaching shoreline. On it was the most magnificent amusement park ever imagined! It extended for miles and miles and in the distance, Jim could hear the laughter of children amid the sounds of the hurdy-gurdy and the clicking wheels of chance.

As they drew closer, Jim saw the Ferris wheel and just like the one he had in his imagination, it had the multi-colored lights and the word Whateverland written in neon tubing at its center.

Jim pressed his hand to his face. "It's... it's amazing! It is by far the most beautiful thing I have ever seen!"

"Well, you deserve it, Pop." Bob stepped back to let Jim soak it all in.

A moment later, Jim turned. "But what about you, Bob? Where is your Whateverland?"

Bob grinned. "Actually, I'm looking at part of it right now."

Jim pressed his hand to his chest. "Me? I don't get it."

Following a short pause, and in a solemn voice, Bob said, "Remember that... discussion we had? The one where you said you didn't think I realized how much my passing would affect you and the family?"

Jim's face turned grim. "It was a stupid comment and something I never should have said."

"And I said, that although my passing would be difficult to deal with, you were only losing one person, while I was about to lose everyone I ever loved and regardless of whatever heaven or paradise awaited me, I couldn't possibly enjoy it if I couldn't enjoy it with the people who meant the most to me."

"So you never…?"

Bob shook his head. "I couldn't see the sense."

Jim smiled and slid his hands into his pocket and drew in the aromatic sea air. "Well, if a crabby old coot like me rates something as magnificent and awe-inspiring as Whateverland, then what you've got waiting for you must be unimaginably beautiful."

Bob shrugged, "Well, I certainly hope so. But a fair bit of warning, if it turns out to be a broken down condo in a lousy neighborhood I'm saying nuts to that and moving in with you!

As the ship pulled into dock and Cap'n Spaulding began tying her up, Jim said, "Son, nothing would make me happier!"

As Jim and Bob left the boat and approached the giant gates of Whateverland, Bob turned to his father and said, "I don't know if you remember saying this to me, but one time when I was a kid, and was down in the dumps, I asked you if we could go get an ice cream sundae or something to cheer me up."

"You said,'Okay,' but on the way you told me that the surest way for someone to make themselves happy, was to start by making someone else happy."

At that moment, the giant gates of Whateverland opened and Jim got his first glimpse at the teeming crowds of people having a wonderful time. Smiles and laughter were everywhere. Families hugging and holding hands, children playing, and teens shrieking with excitement as they enjoyed the many rides and games.

As Jim and Bob entered, Bob stealthily slipped behind his father and as the people in crowd saw him, a round of spontainous applause erupted as he was mobbed by well-

236

wishers and those wanting to thank him for this most wonderful of places.

Amid all the excitement Bob whispered to his father. "If what you said about making other people happy is true, then right now you must be the happiest man ever!"

As Jim wiped away a tear of joy, he said, "Oh I am, son. I truly am."

Chapter 32

"It was a lovely service," Elle remarked to her sister as they walked among the crowd and down the stairs of the small stone 19th century church. They were wearing fall clothes, Anne a knee-length red coat with a beige scarf and Elle an aline blue topcoat. There was a distinct nip in the air. Fallen leaves swirled at the bottom where the two sisters stopped and chatted with those who had been in attendance, thanking them for their kind words and condolences.

Mrs. Tuttle said some lovely words about Jim during the service as did several others who had come to pay their respects.

As the crowd thinned, Anne and Eleanor made their way toward the parking lot.

Anne glanced back at the church. "I was surprised at how many people showed. I didn't realize Dad had that many friends."

Elle nodded.

Several seconds passed before Anne reopened the conversation. "I suppose you'll be getting right back to work now that the funeral's over."

Elle shook her head. "No. I resigned from Goldenrod yesterday and accepted the job at World Traveler. I will start in their Manhattan office in two weeks."

With a puzzled expression Anne said, "I thought you said you were going to think it over. Weigh the pros and cons, you know, that sort of thing."

Elle smiled and placed her arm inside her sibling's. "I was, but when I told Elliot the other day that I would be attending my father's funeral this morning, he became so pissy and unpleasant, I asked myself, 'Why am I working

238

for such a miserable jerk?'" She paused for a moment, then said, "Watching Dad go through his illness reminded me how short life is and how important it is to keep soul-sucking misanthropes like Elliot Chase at arm's length. I have a good life. I have friends, hobbies, interests, and the most wonderful sister in the world. So I decided I wasn't going to let that poor excuse for a human being make me miserable."

Elle shot a questioning glance at her sister. "Now what about you, slick? Still going through with early retirement? What about your swanky DE-LUX apartment in Albany?"

Anne gathered her long hair and pulled it free from inside her coat. "Actually, I'm moving out at the end of the month. Going to bring my stuff here and move into our old house. If you don't mind, that is."

Elle began rummaging through her purse for her Nicorette gum. "Why would I mind? I'll be living in Manhattan, meeting wealthy, eligible bachelors. Handsome, rugged, powerful men, mad with desire for beautiful, alluring women like me. I'll be awash with passion, romance… SEX!"

Anne smirked. "Really?"

Elle sighed as she found the gum and popped one from the foil. "More likely I'll be working fourteen hour days for the first two years and then fifteen hour days as they groom me for the CEO post. I'll probably wind up like Miss Havisham in *Great Expectations*. A rich old bat walking around the house in a worn-out wedding dress, followed by a gaggle of ugly cats. But seriously," Elle said, "why would you want to live in our old house? Why don't you just sell it and use the money to travel the world. You know, live a little?"

"No!" Anne replied. "That's exactly what I don't want. I have spent my whole life doing what was expected of me, excelling at this, exceeding at that, going from one exciting adventure to another. Being Danger Dan and all that crap. And you know what?"

With a smile, Elle stopped, popped the Nicorette into her mouth and said, "What?"

"I'm sick of it!" Anne said firmly. "I'm sick of making the grade, winning the prize, and saving the day. I've decided that from now on I'm going to do what I want to do!"

"And what's that?"

"I'm going to start my own business."

Now it was Elle's turn to say, "Really!?" in stunned surprise. Her car was parked to the right, but she continued walking alongside her sister to hear the rest of the plan. "And what *kind* of business may I ask, pray tell?"

Anne hesitated, then said very quickly, "I'm going to turn all that acreage in the back of the house into an organic farm. Grow vegetables and spices and berries and sell them to local restaurants."

Anne stopped and eyed Elle, expecting an immediate condemnation. When it didn't come, Anne added, "You probably think it's a stupid idea."

"I didn't say that!" Elle tersely replied as she buttoned her coat. "Actually, considering the growth of the town over the last few years and all the new motels, new restaurants and bed and breakfasts, you might do very well."

Anne's mood lightened. "I'm relieved you think so. And remember, since you own half the house I would be sharing half the profits with you."

Elle immediately waved a dismissive hand. "The hell you will! In fact, the first thing tomorrow, I'm going to sign my half of the house over to you!"

"Oh Elle," Anne protested. "That wouldn't be right. I couldn't accept your share."

Elle scoffed. "I'm not giving it to you, I'm dumping it on you. Do you have any idea how important I is right now? I is very important! And if you intend to become some goofball, hippy, earth mother, I can't risk having my sterling reputation as an astute businesswoman take a hit when the FBI shows up, arrests you and your stoner friends and hacks down all your pot plants!"

"C'mon! You know I don't smoke pot."

Elle patted her sister on the back. "Well, it's never too late to start."

As they continued through the church parking lot and approached Anne's car, Elle said, "So you're really going to go through with it? You're really going to bury Dad's ashes next to Bob's in the back yard?"

"Yep!" Anne replied as she pulled her keys from her pocketbook, pushed her key fob unlock button and her dark blue Buick Regal beeped twice. "I've always enjoyed their company."

As Anne prepared to enter her car, Elle rushed over wrapped her arms around her sibling, and hugged her tightly. "You're the only real family I have left. The only one who's stuck by me through it all. Don't let us lose touch. Call me; visit me. And I'll come see you."

Anne returned the hug and smiled. "Of course we'll keep in touch! We're family, and families should always stick together."

Smiling with tears in her eyes, Elle stepped back and said, "That's right! It will always be you and me and..."

241

Elle stuck out her arm and shaped it as if she were wrapping it around some small person's shoulder, "...and our precious, little brother, Bosco O'Bama the Third!"

Anne tilted her head back and laughed, "You are such a dick!"

Elle smiled, and as she turned toward her Corvette, said, "I'll call you tomorrow."

THE END

Thanks for reading Whateverland. You can help others find and enjoy this book by writing a review on Amazon. Just go to http://amazon.com click on books, type Whateverland in the search box and tell us what you thought.

To find other books by Zackary Richards go to http://amazon.com click on books and type in the search box Zackary Richards or contact the author directly at czarrichards@gmail.com